'So we meet again, pretty doctor?'

Cal continued, 'Have you followed me up here to thank me for saving your life?'

Sophie's lips opened to protest, then shut again as her mind went blank, thrown into confusion by something that flickered like forked lightning in the air between them. Fear dried her mouth momentarily, then she realised it wasn't menace that was tightening her muscles and sending tingling shock-waves through her nerves. But it was something just as primitive!

Having pursued many careers—from schoolteaching to pig farming—with varying degrees of success and plenty of enjoyment, **Meredith Webber** seized on the arrival of a computer in her house as an excuse to turn to what had always been a secret urge—writing. As she had more doctors and nurses in the family than any other professional people, the medical romance seemed the way to go! Meredith lives on the Gold Coast of Queensland, with her husband and teenage son.

Recent titles by the same author:

UNRULY HEART
A DIFFERENT DESTINY
WHISPER IN THE HEART

A SUBTLE MAGIC

BY

MEREDITH WEBBER

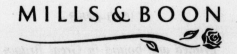

MILLS & BOON

To the members of the original CASSI Committee, who also built a House of Dreams.

*MILLS & BOON, the Rose Device and LOVE ON CALL are trademarks of the publisher.
Harlequin Mills & Boon Limited,
Eton House, 18-24 Paradise Road, Richmond,
Surrey TW9 1SR
This edition published by arrangement with
Harlequin Enterprises B.V.*

© Meredith Webber 1995

ISBN 0 263 14629 4

*Set in Times 16 on 17 pt. by
Rowland Phototypesetting Limited
Bury St Edmunds, Suffolk*

17-9510-49993

Printed and bound in Great Britain

CHAPTER ONE

'I'D LIKE you to tell me the truth, Dr Delano.'

The firm conviction in Mrs Carstairs' voice caught Sophie's wandering attention. She dragged her eyes off the billowing cloud of dust beyond her window and focused them on the woman who sat, hands clasped tightly in her lap, across the desk.

'You'll need to see a specialist, and, because I'm concerned about it, I'll ask the receptionist to make an appointment for you as soon as possible.'

'I thought it didn't look good. It came on quickly, or seemed to! I mean, how often do we look closely at that bottom bit of our legs?'

Sophie smiled at the attempted humour, unaware of how that quick flash of gleaming white teeth lightened her rather sombre oval face and pushed unexpected dimples into her cheeks.

'I think you'd have noticed it if it had been there for any length of time. Getting on to it quickly means you'll have a far greater chance of a complete cure.'

'What kind of chance?'

The patient's blue eyes caught and held hers, and Sophie shook her head. After a day that had presented nothing more worrying than a child with a persistent cough, her examination of the unevenly pigmented, irregularly shaped spot on Mrs Carstairs' leg had thrown her into confusion.

'It's what is called a superficial spreading melanoma,' she explained, hoping her voice sounded more confident than she felt. 'It is the most common of the three types of melanoma, and is a fast-developing malignancy.'

'So we do something about it right away!'

'We do!' Sophie agreed, thankful that her patient was both sensible and co-operative. 'The specialist will explain what he intends to do. He will remove it and have a biopsy done immediately, and may also remove part of the adjoining lymph system, depending on the results of the biopsy. Nowadays, most surgeons use a laser scalpel, which leaves a cleaner wound and causes less bleeding.'

'And after that?'

Again the anxious eyes probed Sophie's.

'It will depend.' She spoke slowly and deliberately, knowing that patients needed time to absorb what they were hearing. 'He may suggest radiation therapy, in case any malignant cells were missed. He may make arrangements for you to have a complete body scan, to check that there are no signs of secondary tumours.'

'And if there are?'

Sophie sighed. She encouraged her patients to ask questions because she believed that knowing what was wrong with their bodies was the first stage in working towards a cure. The hard part was telling people that she didn't know all the answers!

'There is treatment,' she responded evenly. 'It may be long and drawn out, and it may involve unpleasant side-effects, but never lose sight of the fact that many cancers can be cured, and those which can't be conquered can be held in remission for years.'

She smiled again at the woman who sat across the desk, admiring her composure, and seeing a determination in her face that would stand her in good stead whatever lay ahead.

'So much depends on your attitude,' she added, knowing that here was a patient she could trust to be a fighter. 'Go off to the specialist confident that you can beat it, whatever he finds!'

Touching the desk button on her phone with one finger, she stood up to walk with Mrs Carstairs to the door. When Kate appeared in response to her call, she explained quickly and quietly what she wanted done, then showed Mrs Carstairs to a seat in the waiting-room.

'Kate will let you know where to go and what time, as soon as she's made the appointment. You have the referral?'

The other woman nodded, then reached out to grasp Sophie's hand.

'I'm glad you're the doctor I saw today. May I ask to see you 'specially next time I come?'

'Of course,' Sophie assured her, 'but I work odd hours so you'll have to ring and find out when I'm on duty then ask for me when you come in.'

The near-new twenty-four-hour clinic had twelve doctors employed on a roster basis, and patients were usually allocated to whichever doctor was free. While the system lacked the ongoing personal contact with patients that Sophie was aiming for in general practice, it was an excellent way for a newly qualified doctor to gain essential experience.

She walked back into her light, bright consulting-room, and was immediately thankful that the air-conditioning meant she did not have to open the windows. Beyond them, the dust cloud thickened and she fancied she felt the ground shift beneath her feet.

Distant machinery screamed a raucous protest that made the blood freeze in her veins, then her feet started moving before her mind registered the accident her eyes had seen.

'Call an ambulance,' she told the astonished girls at the front desk as she scooted out of the door and around the side of the building, clambering over the chain-wire fence that surrounded the construction site with an awkward urgency.

Her eyes found and remained fixed on the dull yellow bulldozer, resting uneasily on its side halfway up the hill.

The dust was thickest there, but, from the blurred shape, she was certain the cabin was crushed against the trunk of the massive gum tree which had halted its rolling tumble down the slope.

'Stay back, you fool,' a stentorian voice bellowed, but she had no time to check if whoever was talking meant her. Her feet flew on, up the hill towards the crashed behemoth, until, suddenly, she was caught from behind and lifted off the ground, clamped against a rock-hard chest by an arm that felt as if it had sinews of steel.

She kicked her feet and twisted desperately, trying to squirm out of the imprisoning grasp, while the bits of her body in contact with her attacker burned with a fierce, all-consuming heat.

'Put me down,' she gasped, hearing her own voice coming from a long way off, as she struggled for breath, and freedom.

The chest against which she was clasped moved, and she heard a deep-throated growl of denial as her captor carried her back down the way she had come, and flung her unceremoniously back over the fence.

'And hold her if she tries to cross this fence again!' the bossy creature ordered. The small crowd of interested onlookers by the fence had forgotten the crippled vehicle and were peering at her with unabashed amusement. She felt the hot colour of embarrassment creep into her cheeks, and lifted trembling hands to smooth her short dark cap of hair.

'The man in that bulldozer could be badly injured,' she yelled after the man as he moved swiftly away, 'and you're preventing medical help getting to him.'

'I'm more interested in preventing another accident,' he responded crisply, half turning to glare at her for a moment as he stalked up the fence-line towards the top of the slope.

Sophie felt her anger turn to alarm. The man had the coldest grey eyes she had ever seen, and they had cut into her as cleanly and deeply as the laser scalpel she had been telling Mrs Carstairs about.

Although he was receding rapidly, now nothing more than a broad back and dark head against the settling dust, her gaze remained fixed on him, mesmerised by something she could not define.

'They're getting chains. Must be going to try to right it,' one of the onlookers said, bringing her attention back to the accident. Sophie watched the man-mountain who had treated her so roughly join the group of figures at the top of the hill, pause for a moment, then set off, with his purposeful stride, down towards the twisted vehicle.

The ambulance was approaching, its strident warning growing louder as it drew near, but her attention was riveted on the man who was walking steadily down the slope, a huge cable slung across his shoulder and dragging behind him on the ground.

As he neared the crashed machine, she felt the earth move again, and cried out as the tree which had caught the toppling 'dozer groaned and quivered, then flung itself towards the ground with a tearing, agonised fury, right across the track she had been taking before the big man had seized her in his arms.

She shuddered and closed her eyes for a moment, then opened them warily, knowing she had to know what had happened to both the vehicle and the would-be rescuer. Had he managed to attach the cable before the tree fell? she wondered, seeing the machine still motionless on the slope.

'He got it,' one onlooker announced triumphantly.

'No, the roots are holding it,' another argued. 'It could go any moment.'

Sophie held her breath, not understanding why she should be so caught up in the drama unfolding on the slope that her breathing was shallow and fast and her pulse tumultuous.

Fine doctor you're going to make if any emergency brings you out in goose-bumps, she chided herself. She should go back into the clinic, but she was unable to leave the little group of watchers.

There was movement in the dust, then the big man's bulk separated from the machine and he waved his arm in some kind of signal. A mechanical roar sounded at the top of the hill, the cable lifted and strained. Sophie tensed, then saw the bulldozer slowly right itself, its tracks thumping back on to the ground with yet another earth-trembling thud.

Now she broke away, clambering back over the fence but following its line as the man had done, so that she could approach from above the accident, not below it. Higher up, she could see two ambulance men making a cautious descent yards away from the taut cable that held the crumpled machine steady on the steep slope.

Near by, the bulky figure of the big man stood like a statue, peering into the entrails of machinery with a stillness that made her stomach clench with dread.

'I told you to stay over the fence!' he roared as she started to pick her way across the tumbled scree.

'I'm a doctor, I can help!' she yelled back, aware that others were moving down the hill—men with chains and cables to provide more stability.

'No one can help!' he shouted bleakly, although she was now close enough to see him clearly and would have heard him if he'd spoken softly! 'Go back and look after the living.'

An angry frown knitted his black brows into a band across his forehead, and his mouth set in a grim line. There was something shuttered—remote—about his face— something bleak and frozen!

The cold grey eyes seemed to connect with hers, holding her transfixed for a moment while messages she couldn't fully believe flashed into her brain.

The man must be dead! That was what he was telling her. Yet she could read other things, because she had seen that kind of look before.

Go away, those eyes were saying. You don't belong here. You're useless, different. Go back to where you come from.

She turned away. Was she imagining things? Had she become super-sensitive because of messages she'd received time and time again as an immigrant child growing up in a strange country?

A pudgy, dark-haired, dark-eyed little girl, with a sallow olive skin, she'd grown to hate her image and learnt to turn away from the mirrors that repeated it to her so insistently.

Unthinking words and curious looks had tortured her in childhood, leading her to seek refuge in food, so that she'd been fat as well as 'foreign'. Yet, later, she'd turned them to good account, for they had also spurred her on to succeed, to make a place for herself where she would belong.

Defeat pressed down on her shoulders like a heavy weight, yet, for a moment, she hesitated.

'You're certain?'

'Of course I'm certain,' he said abruptly. 'Now get right away from here so the men can stabilise this thing. If that hawser breaks it will plummet to the bottom of the slope, and who knows what damage it might do down there?'

'I should see him,' she protested, peering uncertainly down into the tangled undergrowth. There were houses beyond the scrub, but whether they were on the lower slope of the hill or on the flat ground beyond it she could not recall.

'Get off the hill before I carry you off— again!' he yelled, waving his fist threateningly in the air. She retreated slowly backwards, watching the rescue scene unfolding before her eyes, hoping that the machine could be stabilised before it carried the bossy stranger away with its force, killing another man who had dared to presume he could control it.

A sharp stab of horror pulsed through her and she shook her shoulders irritably, as if to shake away the thought.

Why should she worry about him?

Because he was another human being, and she was trained to help people live, not watch them throw away their lives with stupid acts of bravery.

Her mind's argument brought her safely

back to the fence. She turned away from the drama and hurried back into the clinic, finally aware that her next patient would be waiting.

'His asthma's getting worse and worse.'

He was a small, blond boy of about five, half hidden in the folds of his mother's skirt as that forceful woman dragged him into Sophie's room, explaining volubly at the same time.

'He had whooping cough when he was a baby, although he'd already had his triple antigen. The other doctor thought it might have left a weakness. He's OK for a while, then, as soon as he gets the least bit sick, it starts up again—cough, cough, cough, cough, cough, all night. Drives us mad, and all the dust around this place doesn't help. You'd think the council would make these developers clear all the land they want before they build any houses, instead of choking us all by digging up every tree around the place the moment they run out of house blocks.'

Sophie took advantage of the stream of words to kneel down by the small boy and coax him forward so that she could lift him on to a chair. Warming the end of her stethoscope in her hands, she pushed up the little striped T-shirt, and spoke soothingly as she pressed the disc of metal to his chest.

'Have you noticed any particular foods that might trigger an attack?' she asked his mother as she listened to his chest and picked up the tight wheeze, and the rattle of mucosal oedema.

'Foods?' The question obviously puzzled the woman. Mrs Fraser, Sophie surmised, remembering the name on the child's meagre file.

'Asthma sufferers are often allergic to air-borne pollutants, to household furnishings, cleaning agents, and certain components in food. If we can isolate at least some of the allergens, then we should be able to decrease the incidence of attacks.'

Even as the words left her mouth, she mentally kicked herself for her choice of vocabulary. Hadn't she always sworn to explain things clearly to her patients—not talking down to them, but without using words that could confuse or frighten them? And here she was speaking exactly like a textbook.

She picked up an airflow metre and

snapped on a new mouthpiece, still explaining about food allergies.

'I could refer you to a specialist who would do a series of allergy tests, if you like.'

Both mother and child looked fearful.

'The tests wouldn't hurt much, William,' she said quickly. 'A few little pricks on your arm. But for now I want you to take a deep breath then blow as hard as you can into this,' she explained, handing him the little machine.

'His asthma's not that bad,' Mrs Fraser protested, contradicting her earlier contention with a blithe indifference, while William went bright red in the face from the exertion of producing his best effort.

'Asthma can be fatal,' Sophie warned bluntly, reading the poor forced expiratory volume that he had produced. It was less than half what she would have expected from a healthy five-year-old. 'You should always remember that and take all the precautions you can to prevent attacks.'

The little boy settled comfortably in the chair, his big blue eyes fixed on Sophie's face with the kind of trust that was only found in young children.

'I'm going to give you a puff of Atrovent in one of these spacers, so you can take your time breathing it in,' she explained to him, setting another clean mouthpiece on the clear plastic bubble. 'Later on you can have another blow and see if you get a better score.'

She squirted a metered dose of the drug into the spacer and handed it to him, watching the practised way he inhaled the medication before she turned back to his mother.

'If you don't want him to have the tests at this stage, you could start testing him with different food substances yourself. To begin, let's write down what you can remember happening over the last week. What he's eaten, where you've been, and when he's had attacks. We make a kind of diary, and, if you keep it up to date, after six or eight weeks we should be able to work out a pattern.'

Mrs Fraser shook her head dubiously.

'In six weeks you'll be gone. This clinic's only been open two months and already the first lot of doctors are gone and new ones have taken their place. You never get to see the same person twice—I think that's part of the problem. No one follows through on anything.'

Sophie smiled sympathetically. She recognised that the woman was attacking the clinic in reaction to what she saw as an attack on her mothering.

'I'm not going anywhere for at least a year, and I'll be wanting to follow through on this case. You can see me if you ring and ask for a specific appointment,' she assured her. 'Now, tell me how he's been this week, and maybe William will remember what games he's been playing with his friends.'

With patience, she led the pair through their week, noting down the days when the child's attacks had been most severe, then patiently back-tracking to see if there was any obvious cause or trigger.

'It could take a couple of months for a pattern to emerge,' she said cheerfully, 'especially with food allergies, as traces can linger in his system long after he's stopped eating the particular food.'

Receiving only a grunted reply, she continued, 'It may be a perfectly ordinary thing like dairy food—milk or cheese—that's aggravating William's asthma, and yellow food colouring is another common trigger.'

Mrs Fraser looked disbelieving, and Sophie was aware of a defensiveness behind her attitude. She searched for the right words to convince the woman without implying any criticism.

'Children don't come complete with reference manuals listing their likely allergies, do they?' she said with understanding warming her voice. 'It's up to the poor parents to try to figure it out. May I suggest you take him off dairy products first, and keep a note of the attacks? Continue to use the preventative medicine, and only resort to Ventolin if he's coughing badly.'

Should she tell this uncertain woman that experts suspected misuse of inhalants was contributing to asthma deaths? Not yet, she decided, adding her own comments on the visit to the child's file. She noted down the first forced expiratory volume, then took the spacer from William and handed him the airflow metre again, smiling encouragingly as she said, 'Now, I want a really big blow this time, William.'

She watched the little chest swell as he sucked in air, then his face turn pink as he forced it out. She noted down the reading and was pleased to see that it had improved by twenty per cent. Asthma might already have been diagnosed, but she liked to check things out for herself, and the improvement after use of a bronchodilator was marked enough to confirm that he had reversible airway obstruction.

'Will you try to isolate possible food triggers?' she asked, smiling at the silent woman, her eyes pleading for co-operation.

'I suppose so!'

It was hardly a victory, but there was enough conviction in the grudging words to make Sophie feel cautiously optimistic.

'But you should write to the council about the dust around here,' Mrs Fraser added as Sophie walked the pair to the door. 'I'm sure it's that that's making him sick, and they might take some notice of you, being a doctor and all. Bloody developers!' she finished contemptuously as they emerged into the large waiting area, and Sophie found herself nodding in agreement.

'Sophie!'

The distorted cry made her turn quickly, recognising Meegan's voice before she saw the heavy electric wheelchair and its grinning occupant.

'What are you doing here in Westport?'

she asked, amazement colouring her voice as she moved across to embrace her friend.

'Trying to build a house!' Meegan informed her, with a touch of desperation in the words. 'I'm your next patient, by the way, so you can show me into your rooms.'

She doesn't want to talk about it out here, Sophie realised, standing to one side and waving an arm towards her open door. She walked behind the silent electric vehicle as Meegan manipulated it through the door, her thin fingers pushing against the knob that steered it with a tenseness that betrayed the effort of concentration such a simple manoeuvre required.

'You're building here? In Westport?' She perched on the edge of her desk and looked down at Meegan as she asked the question. Last time they'd met, Meegan had been living with her parents in the city, one hundred miles away, and working as a librarian at the university.

'Trying to!'

'What do you mean, trying to?'

'I met this fellow,' Meegan began, and Sophie watched in delight as colour flooded Meegan's thin cheeks. 'He's also disabled, paraplegic after an accident when he was fourteen.'

The words came pouring out, tripping over each other as Meegan tried to make them intelligible enough for Sophie to follow. The dysphasia that disrupted her speech was part of her cerebral palsy, but Meegan usually managed to make herself understood. A lack of oxygen to the brain during her traumatic birth had caused damage to the motor centres of her brain, but, although Meegan's movements and speech were impaired, her above-average mental ability had not been affected.

'Does he come from Westport?'

Meegan shook her head.

'But he's been offered a job here, and he wants it very badly. It will be good for his self-esteem, you know that.'

The words made Sophie chuckle, a deep, rich sound that brought an answering grin from Meegan. It had taken three months of arguing to convince Meegan to go ahead with tertiary studies and qualify as a librarian, at a time when the younger girl had been bitter and depressed. Self-esteem had been one of the prods Sophie had used to goad Meegan into continuing her education.

'And the new university here will need a librarian!' Meegan added. 'It seems getting a job is much simpler than building a house.'

A heavy sigh punctuated the conversation.

'What's the problem with the house?' As she asked the question, she saw Meegan frown, her face twisting with concentration as she sorted out the words she would need for her explanation.

'We bought land in the new estate up on the hill, but we can't get approval to build.'

There was an anguish in the simple sentence that cut into Sophie's heart, and fired her too volatile temper.

'And why not?' she demanded.

'They won't say,' Meegan explained. 'Well, not in any words I can understand.'

She sighed, and Sophie noticed how pale and tired she looked, now that the initial flush of excitement their meeting generated had faded from her cheeks. The defencelessness of her friend fuelled her anger.

'Who has said you can't build?' She stood up, feet apart, hands on her hips, as if girding herself to do battle.

'The developer! His letter didn't say

much. We rang and his secretary said it has something to do with Mark and Gerald and I sharing the house——'

'Mark and Gerald? You mentioned one young man!' Sophie interrupted.

'Mark is the man I mentioned. Gerald is his friend. They met when Mark lived with a foster family after his accident. Gerald has an intellectual disability, but he's very able in a lot of ways, and for Mark and I even to attempt to live together we need someone who is physically capable of helping us.'

'And Gerald is willing to do this?' The prospect was a little overwhelming, even for Sophie, who had pushed Meegan into seeking more and more independence.

'He can't wait! We all had a bit of money, which we put into the land, and we had arranged to borrow what we need to complete the house, but they say we can't build . . .'

The anonymous 'they', Sophie thought angrily.

'It must be because we are disabled,' Meegan was saying. 'I can't imagine any other reason that people would be against our building. Do they think we'll contaminate their exclusive area?'

'But how do they know about your disabilities? You don't send photos when you apply for building permission! All "they" have are your names.'

Meegan sighed again. 'We didn't need to send photos,' she admitted, her pale mouth drooping at the corners. 'We spent weeks looking for the right block of land, and once we found the Ti-tree estate we drove around it for days, trying to decide which piece of land would suit us best. Then, after we'd bought it, we picnicked there every day for a week, making plans and dreaming.'

Her twisted smile sent a shaft of pain through Sophie's heart—and strengthened her resolve to fight.

'Ti-tree is the new acreage estate, isn't it?'

'Yes. We wanted enough space for a few animals, and Gerald is interested in birds, so we only looked at acreage. Ti-tree is close to the university and not far from the factory where Mark has been offered a job. It was ideal.'

The enthusiasm that had shone in Meegan's eyes as she talked about their land dimmed as she remembered the problems they had now encountered.

'Have you got the letter telling you that

approval has been denied?' Sophie asked as anger churned sickly inside her. How dared someone discriminate against Meegan, Mark and Gerald? There was subtle, more personal discrimination against minority groups in most phases of everyday life, but legislation was supposed to protect them against bureaucratic interference like this.

'Here!'

Meegan thrust a much thumbed letter into Sophie's hands, but the bare words of denial made no more sense to her than they had to Meegan and her friends.

A copy of your application for building approval has been passed on to me. I regret to tell you that your plans do not conform with the existing regulations and consequently will not be approved by the council.

'The cold, callous, contemptuous wretch!'

Her eyes scanned the meaningless phrases that ended the letter, and found the bold black pen-strokes slashing across the bottom of the thick white paper.

'Calgary Williams! Calgary? What kind of name is that? Something he made up to go with some image he's trying to create. Look at this paper! And the letterhead! Who'd put a cowboy hat on a letterhead?'

'They call him The Cowboy,' Meegan said in a quavery voice that did little to soothe Sophie's wrath.

'Who calls who The Cowboy?' she demanded with no consideration for grammatical correctness.

'Cal Williams! People call him The Cowboy,' Meegan explained.

'That's probably the nicest thing they call him,' Sophie muttered, staring down at the piece of paper as if it might hold clues to the psyche of the writer. 'Well, Mr Calgary Cowboy Williams, you may have thought you could bully my friends, but you'd better think again.'

She swivelled off the desk and walked swiftly around it to her chair, punching in the phone number at the top of the letter, her fingers shaking with suppressed anger.

'Where are you staying?' she asked Meegan as she waited for the call to be answered.

'Coastside Motel. Do you know it?'

She nodded as an impersonal female

voice murmured, 'Williams' Developments,' in her ear.

'My name is Sophie Delano, and I'd like to speak to Mr Williams.'

The voice produced a cold and formal apology, with the words 'out on the site and not expected back in the office today' the only ones making any sense.

'Then where can I contact him this evening?' she asked, refusing to be put off by this person who protected her boss's privacy and deflected importunate callers.

'I am not at liberty to reveal Mr Williams' private number. Maybe I can help you?'

The question was crisp, as if the speaker had no wish to help but had been forced to offer.

'No, thank you,' Sophie said firmly, unwilling to defuse her anger by speaking to an underling. She said a cool good-bye, and turned to Meegan.

'I wonder where he lives? Surely I can catch him at home!'

'Don't you read the local papers?' Meegan sounded amazed.

'I don't have time to read any papers. If I'm lucky I catch the late news on television, but apart from that I have to rely on my patients telling me what's going on in the world.'

A sheepish grin accompanied the words. Keeping abreast with what was happening in the world was another thing she'd once nagged Meegan about!

'Well, it's the first thing we did when we thought about moving here. We bought the *Westport News* every day for weeks,' Meegan told her. 'And I doubt if there was more than one or two that didn't mention The Cowboy!' she finished drily.

'Is the man so important in the area? Are we tackling the local hero?'

'Local Casanova more like.' Meegan edged the words with distaste. 'It's in the social pages of the paper that he makes his mark—with a different but equally glamorous female on his arm each time.'

'Westport's answer to Don Juan?'

A dislike of the unknown man was building to mammoth proportions in Sophie's breast as she added 'womaniser' to her perception of him.

'So it seems! I'm almost certain I remember it saying "Mr Calgary Williams of Seafish Cove". That's one of the exclusive new areas, isn't it?'

'So exclusive you can't get past the security at the front entrance to the estate without approval from one of the carefully selected and protected residents,' Sophie responded, deciding that finding the man 'out on the site' might be easier than trying to tackle him at home.

'Then what can we do?' Meegan asked, despair tinging her voice.

'You go back to your motel and leave it to me,' came the crisp response. 'But, before you go, was there a professional reason for this visit? Are you OK?'

'Most of the time,' Meegan told her cheerfully. 'But I do want to speak to you about something. I'll make another appointment, as I've taken up enough of your time at the moment.'

'I've time now,' Sophie protested. 'You must be my last patient as I was due to finish my shift an hour ago. I can stay a little later.'

Her eyes scanned Meegan's face as she spoke, searching for signs of strain or pain. Her friend rarely complained, but Sophie was aware of the agony her cramped limbs and too tight tendons could cause.

'No, no, it can wait,' Meegan insisted, a

sudden pinkness in her cheeks making Sophie even more curious.

'Well, see you make another appointment before you leave,' was all she said. 'I'll phone you at the motel as soon as I've tackled Mr Cowboy.'

'You don't have to get involved, Sophie,' Meegan told her anxiously, her head bent as she concentrated on turning her chair.

'I know that!' Sophie countered, hurrying ahead to open the door. 'But I will anyway!'

She grinned, strangely heartened by the challenge that lay ahead. Tackling The Cowboy might ease the unsettled feeling she'd been experiencing lately, as she discovered the inevitable limitations of her knowledge and ability and learned the frustrations that a novice suffered in general practice.

CHAPTER TWO

TI-TREE estate lay on the northern edge of the burgeoning seaside city of Westport. Sophie admired the forethought of the town planners as she drove through the wide, tree-lined streets towards the new area.

Unlike so many coastal towns that grew from a row of untidy holiday shacks into straggling summer havens, Westport had coaxed business into the area, and planned its own development from the beginning. Streets were laid out in patterned curves and parabolas, yet with a symmetry that made it easy for newcomers and tourists to find their way about.

Most of these blocks would have sea views, she mused as she turned into the elaborately grand entrance to Ti-tree estate.

The developed land ran up the foothills of the low range that curved protectively behind Westport, and Sophie was pleased to see that large stands of native scrub had been left on the blocks, in contrast to the complete razing of vegetation that was

35

taking place behind the clinic.

'No one there, miss,' a cheerful voice called to her as she pulled into the car park at the site office. 'The girl drove off about five minutes ago.'

'I'm looking for Mr Williams and was told he was out here,' she said to the man, who had slipped one foot off his bike pedal for balance while he stopped to chat.

'He'd be up at the new section if he's here,' the stranger offered. 'All this lot is sold out, and he's opening more land a bit higher up the hills.'

'Can I drive up there?'

'Sure can.' He climbed completely off his bike and wheeled it closer, then pointed her in the right direction, gesticulating energetically as he illustrated the turns she should make.

If he's one of the neighbours Meegan and her friends hoped to have, I'm certain he'd not object to their presence in the estate, she decided as she drove off. The man's open friendliness warmed her, reminding her that she'd had little contact with anyone but her patients since she'd arrived in Westport a month earlier.

Earth moving equipment parked in a

lay-by told her she was getting close to where new building blocks were being selectively cleared. She parked her little red Alfasud behind a grader, and clambered out, peering around for signs of life.

Maybe the secretary had used 'out on the site' as an easy excuse not to connect her to Mr Williams. The men who drove the machinery would have finished for the day, so it was unlikely that the boss would still be working. There was certainly no one to be seen.

Spread beneath her, she could see the sprawl of the suburbs, then the three- and four-storey buildings of the town centre, and, beyond them, glimpses of sparkling blue water. This new section of the development, stretching up away from the road, would have sweeping views of the coastline, she decided, then glanced at her watch. Although the sun had disappeared behind the hills, there was at least an hour of daylight left. And when had she last had some decent exercise?

Grinning to herself, she crossed the road and scrambled up the steepish bank above it, turning once again towards the view before beginning the climb that would take her to the top of the estate.

By the time she reached the point she'd aimed at, she was hot, sweaty, dirty, and dishevelled, but she spun around and threw her arms wide open, glorying in the purple velvet of the water beyond the few sparkling lights of early evening. At the southern end of Westport beach, the rocky headland that sheltered the entrance to the harbour thrust like a jagged black spine into the sea, and to the north she could see the intermittent flash of the Rockwash lighthouse.

A magical feeling of peace descended on her, and she felt a sense of renewal as she gazed out across the city to the sweep of ocean.

'This is where I'd like to live forever,' she announced to the silent, scented bush.

'It'll cost you eighty-five thousand, land only,' a voice replied, and Sophie screamed, frozen to immobility by a superstitious terror that was as old as time itself.

Her brain was telling her unconvinced body not to panic, that there must be a logical explanation, when a figure detached itself from a large tree-trunk, a darkly moving shadow among the still sentinels of the dusk.

'So we meet again, pretty doctor! Have you followed me up here to thank me for saving your life?'

Sophie's lips opened to protest, then shut again as her mind went blank, thrown into confusion by something that flickered like forked lightning in the air between them. Fear dried her mouth momentarily, then she realised it wasn't menace that was tightening her muscles and sending tingling shock-waves through her nerves. But it was something just as primitive! Something undefinable! Yet instinct told her it was to be feared as much, or more!

'I—I came looking for Mr Williams,' she stammered, forcing herself to look up into his face, although the lancing grey eyes she'd glimpsed earlier were hidden in the early evening shadows.

'But not to say thank you?'

'You're Mr Williams?' she gasped, one flickering glance taking in the formidable size of the man who now stood an arm's length away from her.

'At your service, ma'am,' he announced, sweeping off an imaginary hat and bowing low. 'Definitely at your service and, if the Chinese are to be believed, now responsible for you for the rest of your life!'

'Don't be ridiculous!' she snapped, irritated by the prickly sensation that his presence was provoking. 'And don't bother flirting with me. I'm not the slightest bit interested in men who use women as ornaments to hang on their sleeves.'

'Flirting?' The deep voice found a texture that made her shiver, and he took another step towards her, absorbing all the air from their surroundings so that she had to gasp for breath. 'You haven't much experience if you think that was flirting, Doctor, darling.'

The words crept across her skin like the slither of a satin nightgown, and she stiffened, made tense and wary by whatever it was that was building like a storm between them.

He stepped across the space that throbbed between them and his big hands dropped heavily on to her shoulders, immobilising her even more effectively than her fear had done. A swift movement blotted out the deepening ink-blue of the sky above the hills, then his lips were pressing hard against hers with a harsh hunger that turned her blood to liquid fire.

'You'd know if I was flirting with you,' he said at last, raising his head and stepping back at the same time so that her hands, flying up to strike him, pounded uselessly into the air.

'You're an arrogant, prejudiced, sexist swine! Is that why they call you The Cowboy—b-because you ride roughshod over people and their dreams?' she stuttered, stumbling forward as her fury sought to vent itself in physical punishment, although she knew her puny strength would have little effect against the iron hardness of his broad chest. She had realised during her earlier contact with him that the man's body was as unyielding as the trees among which he had hidden.

'Prejudiced?' He plucked one single word from her denunciation. 'Not prejudiced, Doctor, dear!'

The slithering softness of his voice had been replaced by a harsh, throaty growl!

'Stop calling me that,' Sophie roared, goaded beyond control. 'And if refusing permission for three disabled people to live in your precious development isn't prejudice, I don't know what is! Disability isn't contagious, you know,' she added scornfully, before pausing to draw a deep, replenishing breath.

'Hold it!' His hands flew up in a mocking signal of surrender, but she knew, beyond any doubt, that surrendering was foreign to this man's nature. Although he might pretend, she realised, which would make him doubly dangerous.

'Building permits are handled by the local council!' he continued. 'I would have thought even a hysterical, stupidly impulsive medico would know that!' His words held the destructive power of a boxer's fists, and Sophie flinched but stood her ground.

'Then why was the letter on your letterhead, with your signature scrawled across the bottom? Explain that, mister.'

She glared up at him, although the impact of her fiercest frown would be lost as night crept through the silent bush and made all but the solid bulk of his body invisible.

'Are you saying that some people with disabilities have received a letter from me refusing permission to build on my estate?'

He sounded so incredulous that she hesitated, then remembered that slash of black ink across the bottom of the heartless letter.

'Unless you never read the things you

sign, you must know about it, so don't try that injured innocence act on me,' she countered, digging in the pocket of her skirt to find the offending piece of paper.

He waited, holding his ground so implacably that she fumbled with nervous tension.

'Here,' she said triumphantly, thrusting the letter towards him. 'Just read that and tell me you know nothing about it. This is the end of the twentieth century, you know, and people who are a bit different from the norm are supposed to be accepted as equals. Or has liberation of all kind slipped past you?'

'I thought you were a bit demented earlier, when you charged across that hill without any thought of the consequences,' declared the voice above her as long fingers snaked out and wrested the piece of paper from her grasp. 'Now I'm certain of it, though how you expect me to read in the dark is a bit of a puzzle. Am I gifted with night vision as well as damned by my prejudices?'

Was he toying with her? The unwelcome thought hit her like a physical blow. She was certain she'd heard a suspicion of humour in his words. Anger bubbled through her blood again, but she bit back the retort that threatened to erupt. Whatever she said, he would turn it against her. Better to guard her tongue and let the evidence speak for itself.

'You can read it in the car,' she replied carefully, turning towards the road in the hope that she might find an easy way back down the slope.

'There's a track over here!'

The words rumbled into her ear, and she fought an impulse to ignore them. More than anything else she wanted to put some distance between herself and this man whose physical presence was so unsettling, but getting lost and having to be rescued—by him!—would be worse than putting up with his company on the descent.

She shrugged ungraciously and walked across in the direction he was indicating, then shrank back as he reached out to take her arm and guide her feet towards the indistinguishable path.

'I have no designs on your virtue, Doctor, dear!' he told her in a sardonic tone, reading her withdrawal with an aggravating accuracy. 'As you pointed out, I have more than enough ornaments hanging from my sleeve at the moment.'

His grasp tightened, and he pushed her almost roughly ahead of him, the hand supporting, but enforcing as well. Again a tremor of not-quite-fear ran through Sophie, and she shivered in the balmy night air as she slid and stumbled down the slope.

'This doesn't say whoever it is can't build on the land!' he said wrathfully a few minutes later, after glancing at the letter he'd signed.

Sophie looked at him blankly. She had watched in amazement as he'd folded himself into the passenger side of her small car, and, even now, she was unable to drag her eyes, and her mind, away from the sight of him scrunched into the seat, his long legs protruding, and his shoulders filling all the space she could see.

'It says their plans won't be approved,' she argued stoutly, although her anger had been dulled by other, less easily recognisable emotions. 'How can they build if their plans aren't approved?'

He looked up from the letter, and his eyes scanned her face, the pale light from

the car interior reflecting as glimmers of
silver in their greyness.

'Plans can be changed to meet the regulations, surely?' he asked, in a smooth,
quiet voice just shaded enough by sarcasm
to make her shift uncomfortably.

'And how are these people supposed to
know that?' she demanded, fighting vali-
antly on. 'You certainly didn't make it clear
in your letter. Or was that your intention?
If they thought they couldn't get permission
to build they might sell their land and go
elsewhere! Is that what you hoped?'

The man they called The Cowboy rubbed
a large hand across his forehead, and she
wondered automatically if he had a head-
ache. Her fingers tingled with an urge to
reach out and feel his head, testing for a
slight fever. She tightened them into fists
and waited in silence, certain he was trying
to think of a valid reason why her friends
could not build on his precious estate.

'Look,' he said at last, 'I can't remember
every set of plans I see, and I certainly can't
remember anything in particular about
this letter. Do you know where the site
office is?'

Sophie nodded.

'I passed it on the way up.'

'Then drive back there and I'll go through the files.' His eyes were fixed on her face again, but she couldn't read the expression in them. 'I've a feeling the only way I'm going to get you off my back is to sort out whatever problem it is that your friends are having.'

Now the glittering gaze flickered over her body, drawn up in defiance to her full five feet six. The grey eyes slid up and down with an insolence that made her squirm.

'There's not much of you,' he added, in a voice that sounded like ground glass, 'but I've a feeling every ounce is pure trouble.'

He unwound himself from her car and strode away. A car door slammed, then a dark shadow emerged from behind the machinery, and headlights slashed through the darkness, pinning Sophie, for an instant, in their beam before passing on, leaving only a blacker night. He was well ahead of her by the time she turned to follow, but she recognised the high square body of a powerful four-wheel-drive vehicle.

Lights sprang on in the site office as she parked her car, but she felt no welcome in their glow. Why had she decided to tackle this problem head-on? Wouldn't a letter have sufficed?

Second thoughts kept her huddled in the secure darkness of the car, then the office door opened, light spilling out, illuminating the dark figure who stood, impatience clear in every line of his body, peering into the night.

She pushed open the car door and emerged reluctantly, the urge to pit herself against this intractable man slowly seeping away as tiredness crept through her.

'That plan won't be approved because the area is zoned for single-occupancy dwellings,' he announced as she came towards him.

'You mean only one person can live in each house?'

His face showed the stupidity of her question.

'I mean each block of land will only have one residence on it. This plan shows three units within a single building.'

He was explaining with the exaggerated patience of an adult towards an uncomprehending child.

'And although your friends haven't applied for separate title for each of the units, the council is always wary that plans like this could be the subject of later applications. Why else, they think, would people want to build this way?'

He pulled her into the demountable building that served as an office, his hand on her arm a startling invasion of her personal space, and thrust a roll of paper, half unravelled, into her hands. Sophie looked at the plans, but she could make no sense of the maze of lines and mess of figures.

'See how the architect has designed three specific areas,' he said impatiently, leaning over her shoulder to draw a finger along the lines. He was so close, she imagined she could feel the rise and fall of his chest against her back.

Dismissing the fantasy, she forced herself to concentrate. Each bedroom had an adjoining bathroom, and a small room that could be classed as a sitting-room opening off it. The communal area of the house—a large lounge-room, dining-room and kitchen—were positioned in such a way that they lined up with the three bedrooms and someone—in the council perhaps?—had drawn straight red lines down the plan as if to show the possibilities of dividing the house into three flats.

'It's been planned this way because three people plan to share the house and each of them values their own privacy,' she pointed out, guessing at the motive behind the unusual layout. 'And those rooms all flow into each other in that kind of open-plan space to eliminate the need for a hallway.'

'Are hallways taboo when people share a house?' he asked, the sarcasm she'd suspected earlier now unleashed.

'When two of the three people are in wheelchairs, yes!' she told him defiantly, swinging around to glare at him as she spoke.

It was a mistake. His bent head was on a level with hers, and she was immediately confronted by the sight of firm tanned skin, bluish-black where the beard line shadowed it, an angular jaw, thin straight nose, and grey eyes that, close to, had minute black pin-point marks painted in the grey.

The unusual combination drew her gaze, and she stared, fascinated, into them, until a strange breathlessness brought her back to the present and she spun away, dropping into a chair. Her fingers smoothed at the paper, but her eyes were not focusing, seeing instead a clear vision of cool grey eyes, flecked with black.

'If Meegan writes to the council and explains why the house is planned this way——'

'They still won't pass it! Your friends want to excavate into the slope so they can build on one level, and the covenant on the land states that houses must be built on the natural gradient. That would have been noted on their deed of title.'

He had come close again, but this new objection reminded Sophie why she was here, and her fighting spirit roused again, mixing with the unease that his presence was engendering.

'Split-level housing is fine for able-bodied people,' she said crossly. 'If you enforce that stupid covenant, you're discriminating against people who use wheelchairs.'

'The covenant is there to protect the land from any more degradation than is absolutely necessary,' he informed her. 'For too long builders have bulldozed into the side of hills to provide flat platforms for their foundations, ignoring future consequences like landslips and drainage problems.'

'So, because of past mistakes, these people can't build on your precious estate.' She slammed a hand down on the plans. 'It's discrimination, Mr Cowboy, and that's illegal.'

The force of the words was weakened by the bright colour that swept up into her cheeks as she realised what she'd called him.

'Mr Williams, I mean!' she mumbled, the sincerity of the apology lost in the tightness of her voice as she uttered it, furious with herself for making the mistake.

'Oh, you can call me Cowboy,' he said smoothly, his eyes focusing with an unsettling intensity on her vivid face. 'It's probably better than most of the things you'd like to call me.'

The strange grey eyes continued their scrutiny, adding to her embarrassment. Heat burned through her, and she longed to press her hands to her flaming cheeks, but to do so would be to show a weakness in front of this man, and she was not going to do that!

'If they want to avoid stairs, your friends could raise their house to the level of the back of the land. If they use a simple pole construction system it will cost about the same as the original plans.'

He leaned forward again, his body close enough to warm hers as he drew thick black lines on the plan to demonstrate what he was suggesting.

'Couldn't you have told them that?' she demanded, thoroughly disconcerted by the man's nearness, and by his about-face from adversary to obliging adviser.

'If they'd asked!'

He stood up abruptly, and Sophie shivered, perceptibly chilled, but whether because he had moved or from the tone of his voice she could not decide.

'Would you help them sort out the problems?'

She was startled by her own temerity! Why had she hit the ball back into his court?

'It's a matter of having the plans redrawn,' he informed her in a clipped, distancing voice. 'I'm not an architect or a draughtsman.'

'But you do know what the council wants,' she countered, stupidly disappointed with his reaction. 'Or have you decided you don't want these people living on your estate and you're now looking for someone else to blame for your own behaviour?'

Her eyes met his, warm rich brown challenging mysterious grey. He turned away first, but not before she'd glimpsed the puckering of skin between his black brows as the beginning of a frown darkened his face. Had she ruined the trio's chances of approval by pushing things too far?

'Tell them it's a problem with the plans, and not insurmountable,' he said abruptly, dismissing her from his presence as clearly as if he had opened the door and waved her out.

Rising to her feet, she stepped towards the door, then looked back at the man who stood propped against another desk, his long legs stretching halfway across the floor in the small office. His head was bent, as if earnestly studying his brown riding boots.

'Thank you for seeing me,' she muttered, all composure lost in an uncertainty that she hadn't felt for years.

He nodded, but did not reply, nor lift his head. Sophie hurried out, pleased to escape his disconcerting presence, yet contrarily reluctant to leave. She stepped carefully down into the darkness.

The pathetic wailing of a cat came from beneath the site office, and Sophie forgot the man as she dropped to her knees and called softly.

Was the cat stuck under there?

The noise came from the far side, she decided, clambering back to her feet and moving warily around the building until she reached the spot where the cry seemed loudest. Hissing invitingly, she crouched down again, and was answered by a plaintive mew. Banishing thoughts of snakes and spiders from her mind, she reached out into the darkness beneath the building, and felt the softness of fur, matted and damp, but unmistakably cat.

'Come on, puss, puss!' she called, and felt the animal respond with a convulsive movement.

'What are you doing now?'

He was speaking quietly but his voice still startled her, and she spun around, peering up at him as he stood, feet planted belligerently apart, towering above her like a presentiment of doom.

'There's a cat under here, and I think it's injured.' Why did she sound defensive?

'Probably a feral cat come out of the bush

where we've been clearing. They are a menace and should be exterminated.'

The words had a crisp finality, but something about this man's certainty forced her into argument.

'A feral cat wouldn't let me touch it! I can reach it, but my arms aren't long enough to lift it out.'

He let out an exaggerated sigh, but Sophie ignored it. She would need his help if the cat was to be rescued. Her fingers continued to stroke the bit of the animal she could reach, and the awful wailing had faded to plaintive cries.

When the big man dropped down beside her, a small grin of triumph twitched at the corners of her mouth and she turned away, not wanting him to see it in the light from the trailer windows.

'Where is the damn thing?'

'Just under there!'

She moved aside, letting him take her place, then realised he wasn't feeling in the right direction.

'More this way,' she muttered, drawing closer and taking his hand to guide it in under the shed. She touched other people all day in her profession, yet touching this

man was so different that she had to force
herself to pretend he was another patient.
Beneath her hand, the skin, muscle, sinew
and bone seemed alive, warm, silky soft, yet
strong as steel.

'I've got it!'

He interrupted her thoughts, and pushed
her out of the way as he thrust his other
hand beneath the building. 'I suppose if I
go about inviting spider or snake bite, it's
just as well to have a doctor on the spot.'

As he spoke, he drew back, until his
hands were revealed, holding a marmalade
cat, its coat matted with dark blood, its eyes
already turning to the opaqueness of death.

'You won't be able to save it, but I suppose it was better to get it out before it died
under there.'

The prosaic attitude chilled her, but her
fingers were already running gently over the
animal, feeling the delicate bones beneath
the skin, then finding the crusted lips of the
huge jagged wound.

'Put her down so I can feel her properly.'

'Say please, Doctor, dear.'

Was he reacting to the peremptory way
she had spoken?

'Please, and thank you,' she added, sur-

prised by the gentleness of those large hands
as he lowered the cat's body to the ground.

'Even if you do save her, what will happen? You can't tame feral cats.'

His voice was brusque, and told her,
unmistakably, that he thought her concern
was stupid and irrational.

'She can't be feral! A feral cat wouldn't
seek help from humans! She's been lost then
injured.'

The cat moved as she spoke, shrugging
itself over on to its paws, body crouched
low to the ground, then, in one swift dash,
it was gone, disappearing back underneath
the building.

Sophie felt stupid tears of rejection spring
into her eyes, and she looked at her companion, wordlessly wondering what to do.

Above them, the moon was casting silver
light through the trees, softening the cleared
area where they crouched with its pearly
radiance. Mr Calgary Williams' face was
shadowed, but moonlight gleamed on his
ebony dark hair and caught the corner
of his jaw, illuminating a pulse that
beat strongly in the vulnerable softness
beneath it.

A rustling sound broke the silence

between them, and Sophie looked down to see the cat emerging, inch by inch, until it reached the space between their feet. Something dropped from its mouth, and then it lay down—quiet, and too still.

'Quickly, lift it into the light. I may be able to suture the wound.'

'And start heart massage and a drip? The cat is dead!'

His voice held the same stony acceptance that she'd heard earlier. Reaching out, she felt the small body already cooling, and a momentary sadness swept over her.

'But there's another life to save, Doctor, dear,' the deep voice rasped, then her companion reached out and took her hand, turning it palm upwards, and depositing a small bundle of fur into it.

'She brought her kitten out to us!' she cried, looking into his face with a shy smile of wonder. 'It took the last ounces of her energy, but she brought it out and gave it to two human beings, knowing they would care for it. A feral cat wouldn't do that!'

'A feral cat would have more sense. This human, for one, has no intention of taking care of a kitten that probably can't lap and will need feeding with an eye-dropper.'

'Have you done that before?' She felt surprised at the idea of this huge, strong, overtly masculine man, indulging in such a tender act of mercy.

'Many years ago,' he told her drily, the skin at the corners of his remarkable eyes crinkling just slightly, as if a smile might not be far away. 'And I haven't forgotten how difficult and time-consuming it was, so don't look at me with that soulful Madonna face and think I'll take any part in this cat-rearing exercise.'

Sophie rubbed her fingers against the downy head, automatically soothing the little ball of fluff while she pleaded for its life.

'But I'm living in a rented flat with strict rules forbidding any pets.' Her eyes added an extra plea to the desperation in her voice. 'You can't let the poor wee thing die.' She paused, unable to read his reaction in the moonlight. 'And it is on your property!'

A stillness tightened the air between them, and the bush fell silent. Sophie's gaze remained fixed on the flat planes and sharp angles of his face, searching for a hint of the compassion he would need to take on the task of rearing the tiny kitten.

'Seduced by a pair of pansy brown eyes at my age,' he muttered, and Sophie let her lashes drop, to flutter against her cheeks, embarrassed by the intimacy in his voice and the sudden charging of the atmosphere between them.

'Give it to me and get out of here,' he ground out. 'Quickly! Before I change my mind!'

She dropped the tiny bundle into his outstretched palm, avoiding contact with the skin that stretched palely across it.

'Thank you,' she murmured, straightening up. For an instant she hesitated, then she turned and fled, leaving the man and kitten, a single dark shape in the shadow of the building.

CHAPTER THREE

'I'M GLAD one of our doctors is on time this morning!' Emma, the early-morning-shift receptionist, greeted Sophie with an approving smile.

'It's still easy for me to get up before dawn, as a five o'clock start was a normal part of hospital routine,' Sophie told her. 'It's harder for the older doctors who are working part-time as they ease into retirement.'

'And not hard for older receptionists?' the middle-aged woman responded with a wry grimace, and Sophie acknowledged her remark with an understanding nod.

'It doesn't look as if I'll be rushed off my feet before help arrives, anyway. I don't think I've ever seen an empty waiting-room before.'

'Make yourself a cup of coffee, and take it and the paper into your room. You won't have much time to relax once the patients start arriving.'

Emma pushed the fresh-looking paper

across the desk towards her. It was the *Westport News* and Calgary Williams' grainy image leapt off the front page at her, mocking and sardonic even in a bad black and white reproduction.

'That's the story about the accident they had behind the clinic yesterday,' Emma told her, with a gossip's love of imparting bad news. 'The chap on the 'dozer was decapitated, it says!'

Sophie's fingers trembled on the newsprint, and she pushed the paper back towards Emma, unable to bring herself to read the over-dramatised details that the report would almost certainly contain. The thought of the man losing his life that way made her feel sick. No wonder the would-be rescuer hadn't let her look at him! Yet she was a doctor, trained to assist no matter how horrific the accident. Not that she could have assisted anyway. The thoughts jostled in her mind.

She forgot about coffee, and turned to hurry into her room, disturbed by an uncertainty that was rare in her professional life.

As she gazed out of the window at the fallen tree, an image of the man they called The Cowboy remained fixed in her mind, as

vivid as if he still strode up the hill. The
buzzer, activated when a file was dropped
into the slim box on her door, told her that
a patient was waiting and she dragged her
attention back to the present.

'I'm Martin Dempster,' the young man
told her, shuffling tiredly through the door
with a crying baby in his arms. 'This is
Jancy. She's seven weeks old and she won't
stop crying. My wife's been up all night, and
I've brought her here to you because if she
doesn't stop soon I don't know what
we'll do.'

Red-rimmed eyes told of the sleepless
nights he had endured, and a tightness in
his face and voice were enough to warn
Sophie that he was close to cracking. Lack
of sleep and the aggravation of the constant
noise could produce pressures in even the
most equable parents. It was a dangerous
situation, and she recognised it as such.

'Give her to me,' she said quietly, taking
the whimpering child from his arms and
rocking her gently against her shoulder. The
little bundle felt as tense as her father
looked, and she moved restlessly in Sophie's
arms, drawing up her legs and kicking her
tiny feet against Sophie's breast.

'She's not hot, so infection is unlikely. Is she your first child?'

'And last at the moment,' the father agreed, nodding in a despairing way. 'I know it seems ridiculous that two grown people can't cope with something that size, but we don't know what to do next. I took three months' leave to help Anna with the baby, but she's got us both beaten.'

The whimpering became a piercing bellow of distress as Sophie sat down, so she stood up quickly and continued to pace the floor, patting the squirming infant while she listened to the man pour out his problems.

'We've tried everything we can think of. We've read all the books, and our mothers have both come up with ideas, but nothing seems to work. If she sleeps for an hour between feeds, we celebrate!'

'How often is she fed?'

'Anna started with demand feeding in the hospital, and Jancy's pretty regular now, at about four-hourly. We tried feeding her more often, thinking she might have been hungry, but if she doesn't want to feed she turns away and keeps crying. We pick her up and cuddle her, and carry her around the house, but most of the time that doesn't stop her either. Now we're worrying that she'll never sleep properly, that she'll want this attention all the time, and we won't be able to keep it up.'

Sophie nodded sympathetically.

'There are new theories abounding that wind doesn't exist, but many babies, especially first-born, have this problem. The parents' anxiety that they are doing the right thing could be part of it, but there has to be a physical reason for a child to cry so relentlessly. Colic is the most likely explanation. We think some babies suck in air as they feed, and when this becomes lodged in their bowels it causes pain and they cry.'

'So what do we do?'

The young man was not going to be appeased by explanations. He wanted an instant cure, and it was unlikely that she could provide one.

'What have you tried?' she asked, easing the baby into a more comfortable position on one arm so that she could write on the file without prompting more bellows. She noted down the readily available colic treatments as the young father repeated them, grinning over the 'drop of brandy in a teaspoon of sugar' that one grandparent had suggested.

'I think we've tried everything the chemist stocks,' he said at last, spreading his hands in a despairing gesture.

'I think you have, too,' Sophie agreed, mentally running through possible ways to deal with a problem that was fast getting out of control. 'I can prescribe Donnalix Infant Drops, which act as a depressant on the nerves in the bowel and will stop the spasms, but there is a limit to how much Jancy could take in one day, so you would have to decide which feeds usually produce the worse symptoms, and use the medication sparingly before those specific feeds.'

'What would happen if it were used more often?'

'The main ingredients are derivatives of belladonna, which is a poison, so an overdose could be extremely serious. Dosages are based on body weight, so you will understand that a few drops too much in a baby Jancy's size could be fatal, while a dessertspoon-full for someone your size could be an appropriate dose.'

The young father nodded, a frown gathering between his eyes as he thought through what Sophie was telling him.

'That's a pretty risky thing, then,' he muttered, and Sophie nodded.

'And a lot of extra responsibility and anxiety for you and your wife,' she agreed, hoping he was concerned enough to accept her next suggestion.

'Although the infant drops are a very weak solution, and it would be harder than you think to give Jancy an overdose, it is always better if they can be administered in a situation where they can be controlled. Have you heard of Somerset House?'

A quick shake of his head answered her question, and she continued swiftly, knowing she had his interest, 'It's a different kind of clinic set up by the Maternal and Child Welfare Department, where parents can live in with their infants while problems like this are sorted out.'

Watching the flicker of unease in the young man's face, she hurried on.

'You and your wife would have a private room and bathroom, with a little room off to one side for Jancy. All the bedrooms open out on to a wide veranda and the house is set in beautiful gardens. Meals are provided in a central dining-room and you can come and go as you would at a motel, doing as much or as little for Jancy as you wish.'

'Who would look after her, if we weren't doing it?' The question was loaded with suspicion.

'The house is staffed by nurses with specialty training. Sometimes a mother might stay for a few weeks while the staff help settle the baby into a sleeping pattern, or establish successful breast-feeding. All rooms have double beds, and where possible we encourage the father to stay with his wife, even if he has to go to work from Somerset. In Jancy's case, the staff could take care of her between feeds, so that you and your wife are not distracted by her crying, and can catch up on some much needed sleep. They could also experiment with the amount of Donnalix she needs to ease her pain, and sort out her sleeping problems before you take her back home.'

She was pleased to see the interest in his face, but she couldn't push the suggestion too far, so rose to her feet and walked across to the window, rocking back and forth to soothe the fretful baby.

'But what would that cost?'

'It's a free service,' she said quietly, turning to face him. 'The powers-that-be realised a long time ago that it was better to spend money on solving these problems early than on patching up families after help came too late. A nursing sister who believed that all infant problems could be sorted out with time and patience left her house to be used specifically for this purpose and the government agreed to fund the staffing.'

'Are the meals free?' he asked, still suspicious of what must seem like a dream solution to his problems.

'There's a small charge, if you can afford it, but people who cannot pay are just as welcome. I'll ring Somerset and tell them you might be interested, and give you some papers about the place to take home and show your wife. If you decide to go ahead with the idea, you will have to phone them and arrange accommodation.'

'They might be full!' he said, as if unwilling to give up his seemingly insurmountable problem quite that easily.

'If they are, they will probably be able to provide someone to come and live in with you until a vacancy comes up. That way, you'll have an extra pair of hands to help at home——'

'And an extra pair of legs to walk the little monster at night!' he interrupted, and there was enough affection in his voice when he spoke of his 'monster' to reassure Sophie that the situation could be remedied.

Ignoring Jancy's protest, she crossed to her desk and sat down again, pulling open the deep filing drawer by her side and searching through for the information she wanted.

'Here you are! Take it home and talk it over with your wife.'

He took the booklet and rose to his feet, reaching out for his baby. Relief showed his features in a softer light.

'I'll let you know what we decide,' he said gratefully. 'I'm certain Anna won't mind being woken up to hear about this!' he added, waving the papers over his shoulder as he strode to the door.

As the door opened, she saw the next file stuck in its box, and followed the young father, stopping to retrieve the file and looking around the waiting-room to identify her next patient.

'Mr Ambrose!' she called, and had barely

said the name when a tall, now too familiar figure uncurled itself from the depths of a leather armchair and came towards her.

'You're not Mr Ambrose,' she said shortly, backing into her room and resisting an urge to slam the door on his encroaching form.

'Don't you want me for a patient?' he asked softly as he approached with unfaltering steps.

No! something shrieked inside her. Not now, and not ever!

The thought of seeing this man as a patient—of trying to examine even the most innocuous bit of him, like his big toe—made her shiver with a premonitory agitation.

'Relax,' he continued, forcing his way inexorably through her half-open door. 'I'm here with one of my workmen. The nurse is cleaning the wound and will bring him in to you shortly. I thought, in the meantime, you might like to see your protégé in daylight.'

He reached into his jacket pocket, which, she now saw, was bulging in a strange fashion. A cylinder of cardboard had been cut to form a short but solid semicircle and shoved into the material to prevent the tiny ball of fur he now produced being squashed against his body.

'I didn't expect you to nurse it constantly,' she said, accepting the tiny ginger-coloured kitten in her cupped hands and lifting it to rub the downy fluff against her cheek.

'If you heard the noise it makes when it's left on its own, you'd understand,' he said gruffly, and Sophie looked up, astonished by the intimation of softness in this man she'd thought of as rock-hard. Grey eyes glinted in his tanned face, but no glimmer of a smile suggested he might be joking. Sophie's stomach turned over. Something about Calgary Williams caused a physical reaction that she was powerless to control, yet she didn't think she was afraid of him.

'Naughty puss,' she admonished, swiftly switching her gaze from grey to golden eyes, which stared as unblinkingly at her. 'You'll have to learn to behave better than that, or Mr Williams will be sorry he adopted you.'

'I adopted it?' he queried sarcastically. 'I had no intention of adopting it. It was forced on me by a silly, sentimental woman who was quick enough to find an excuse why she couldn't keep it herself!'

The arrival of her patient prevented further argument, and Sophie turned to greet David Ambrose with a smile, before handing the kitten back to Calgary Williams and crossing to the small sink to scrub her hands. She dried them carefully, then pulled on disposable gloves.

'Are you staying to hold his hand?' she asked him as she helped the patient—a burly middle-aged man in the hard-wearing clothes of a labourer—up on to her couch.

'I'm here to see his injury is properly treated,' he told her, rejecting her taunt with menacing tones. 'Left on his own, he'd have sneaked off home, put three strips of plaster across it, and come back to work. I've seen him ignore wounds before and end up in hospital.'

With a gentle sureness, she rested the injured hand on a small stand she had fitted to the edge of the couch, and lifted the cotton wadding which the nurse had used to cover the wound. Although she was concentrating on what had to be done, part of her mind was wondering at the consideration of this particular boss. Did it fit with the image of a man who was being deliberately obstructive towards her friends?

'It's a messy kind of injury,' she announced as she examined the ragged edges of the tear and probed at the bits of black grit still visible in the wound.

'Grabbed at a chain that was moving,' came the laconic reply. David Ambrose cast an apologetic look at his boss, then added, 'And I know I should have known better but I couldn't guess that the idiot driver was going to take off before I'd finished checking the gear.'

There was a grunt of acceptance from the onlooker.

'I'm going to wash it again with a saline solution,' Sophie told her reluctant patient, 'then try to pick out all the bits of foreign matter. When did you last have a tetanus injection?'

The man went pale at the words, and his minder nodded.

'I told you he was a coward. It's probably years, and even then they'd have had to give him a general anaesthetic before they could administer it.'

'I had one about ten years ago,' David Ambrose muttered defensively.

'Then you'll need a booster,' Sophie told him crisply, continuing to pick bits of metal out of the torn palm of his hand. 'Now turn your wrist.'

She watched as the man moved the injured hand.

'This time close your fist.' The movement was free and natural, allowing for a slight protectiveness of the badly gashed palm.

'Do this,' she ordered next, touching her thumb on to each of her fingers in turn. 'Great!'

'And what does that mean?' her onlooker asked.

'It means there's no tendon damage, and that the wound, though nasty, is fairly shallow.'

She would have liked to add a sardonic, Satisfied? but professionalism made her bite her tongue. She mustn't let this man upset her. Once she had fixed his friend's hand, she need never see him again.

She concentrated on her patient, digging a glove-coated fingernail into the tip of his thumb.

'Feel that, did you?' she said with a smile as he tried to withdraw his hand. 'And this?' She repeated the procedure on the tip of each finger, checking for any loss of feeling.

'Now that I know there is no motor or

nerve damage, I'm going to give you a local anaesthetic then use absorbable sutures to fix the deep tissue damage.'

She nodded to the nurse who had been hovering by the door, who disappeared from the room, returning a little later with two syringes, swabs, two ampoules of drugs and a multi-dose vial in a kidney bowl. Sophie acknowledged her silent presence with a smile, and picked up the vial of Xylocaine, checking the five per cent concentration marking on the slender glass tube as she drew up the solution into the first syringe.

'Are you allergic to anything that you know of?' she asked the patient, her quick gaze running down the notes the receptionist had made on the new file.

'Only injections,' the burly man replied with an exaggerated shudder.

'Are you on any medication at all, or taking any non-prescriptive drugs like cold tablets, antihistamine or pain-killers?'

A swift shake of his head answered the question and she swabbed his wrist and inserted the needle so swiftly that he had no time to try to twitch away from her grasp.

'That's one,' she said, reinserting the

needle to deaden the ulnar nerve, 'two to go.'

Her patient groaned but held his hand still.

'We'll leave the tetanus till later,' she said with a smile as she rubbed the injection site to disperse anaesthetising liquid through the tissues, watching her patient carefully for signs of an adverse reaction. A total of thirty ccs would deaden the pain long enough for her to clean up the wound and suture the soft tissues.

Satisfied that he was stable, she completed the injections to provide a wrist bracelet block, then turned her attention back to the wound. Shaking her head in dissatisfaction, she glanced up to see The Cowboy's eyes watching her fixedly.

'I'll suture the inner tissues, but I'm not happy about closing such an untidy wound in case infection develops beneath the sutures; but if Mr Ambrose won't rest that hand until it heals, there'd be less risk of permanent injury if I close it.'

'I'll see that he rests it!' the younger man declared, glaring with mock-severity at his employee. 'Even if I have to tie him to a chair.'

'Worried about the compensation claim, boss?' the patient teased, while Sophie took advantage of the diversion to snip away the ragged edges of the tear.

'I'll close the skin with butterfly strips. If no infection develops, they will be nearly as good as sutures in drawing the healing edges together.'

'What about antibiotics?'

The big man followed her to the small cabinet by the wall, and slouched above her while she changed her gloves then chose thread and needle, releasing each from its sterile packet with exaggerated care as she tried to ignore him.

Who's the doctor here? she felt like asking, but again resisted the temptation to fight him.

'I'll give him broad spectrum antibiotics, but with open wounds there's no way of knowing what might have got in, so there's always a risk.'

'And what if it becomes infected?' he persisted, following her back to the table like a particularly irritating fly.

'If left unchecked, it could cause damage that would limit mobility in the hand. That's why I am not closing the wound, Mr

Williams, and why I shall insist on seeing Mr Ambrose daily for the next few days.'

He ignored the tetchiness in her voice, merely aggravating her further with a murmured, 'I liked Mr Cowboy better!'

Satisfied that he had had the last word, he crossed the room and leaned against the wall by the door, his arms folded across his broad chest, and a gleam of malicious enjoyment in his pale eyes.

'You won't feel this,' she murmured to her patient, then drew together the torn scraps of tissue, stretching them tightly in an attempt to minimise the risk of adhesions forming later.

'Don't forget his tetanus shot!'

Sophie was startled. She had managed to ignore Calgary Williams while she'd concentrated on her work, but as she fastened the pristine white bandage around her patient's wrist he forced himself back into her thoughts with his reminder.

'This is not the first case I've treated,' she said tartly, keeping her back to him although she could now feel his presence through every nerve that spread from her spine so that her back tingled unceasingly.

With a mammoth effort of will, she

resisted the urge to shrug the irritation away, focusing instead on drawing up the tetanus antitoxin, and coaxing her patient to remain steady while she injected it. As she watched the colour wash away from beneath the sun-darkened skin, leaving a grey shadow across his face, she understood the man's real fear of injections and patted his arm reassuringly.

'It's all over now,' she told him, speaking quietly and shielding his reaction from Calgary Williams' sight. She could almost hear the man's sarcastic amusement at her patient's fear of needles, and David Ambrose was in no condition to cope with any further teasing.

'I'm just going to put it in a sling to raise it above the level of your heart. It will heal faster if you keep it there and don't use it,' she added severely.

'Can you arrange for Mr Ambrose to go home and rest?' she said crisply to his boss, when she was satisfied that her patient was feeling well enough to move. 'Do you want a certificate saying he's unfit for work or will you allow him the time off?'

What was it about this man that made everything she said to him a challenge? she wondered, hearing the belligerence in her words. She forced herself to look up into his face, her own lips thinned disapprovingly as she waited for an answer.

Massive shoulders lifted in surrender.

'You can give him a hundred certificates telling him he's unfit to work—he'll come back as soon as he's ready.' He had picked up her challenge and flung it right back at her, she decided, but she stood her ground and kept her eyes fixed on his, searching for those tiny shards of black in the greyness.

'Which will probably be tomorrow!' her tormentor added, bringing her back out of a dream of glinting silver eyes.

'Please call in each day and have it dressed.' Sophie turned away and hurried over to where David Ambrose slouched against her couch. 'That way I can check for infection. I'll also give you a prescription for antibiotics. Start with two now then one four-hourly, and you should be fine.'

'Thanks, ma'am!'

Sophie grinned at the laconic reply. A man of few words, she decided—in strong contrast to his boss, who would use words as weapons!

As the pair disappeared through the door,

she wondered where that thought had come from, knowing only that she was certain it was true.

'I'll be back to see you later!'

Had her thoughts conjured him up again? His dark head appeared around the door-jamb, and he threw the comment at her with no introduction or explanation—a statement that did little for her equilibrium as she prepared to get on with her day's duties.

A quick knock on the door heralded Kate and reminded Sophie that it must be later than she imagined, as her favourite among the receptionists never started work before nine. A single mother, she had to organise her children and deliver them to school before she could begin, and her timetable had been adapted to fit in with the children's routines.

'Do you want a coffee?' she asked, smiling at Sophie, her face crinkling with an infectious warmth.

'Love one, if there aren't too many people waiting,' Sophie replied, coming across the room to take the file that Kate was holding. 'If you send this patient in, I'll have coffee when I finish.'

She sat down to read it, but it was another undocumented patient and the file told her little. In such a new area, few patients had medical records. It was part of the demise of the type of general practice that Sophie had experienced in her youth. Her family had gone to the same local doctor from the time they had arrived in this country, and her parents still saw the man who had removed Sophie's tonsils when she was six. Now people moved about so much, they no longer had a family doctor, choosing instead to go to whoever was closest to where they were living at the time—or whoever happened to be open. This was the reason why big clinics like this were so successful, as many people simply wanted convenience and service, not attention— which were two very different things in Sophie's mind.

'He's due for his first triple antigen!'

Must be a day for babies, Sophie thought as she greeted Mrs Warren and her tiny son Joel.

'Mum says he should have one at two, four and six months then another one before he's two and a booster before he goes to school, but my husband doesn't want him having an injection. He read that it can cause problems for the baby, and he won't have that for Joel.'

The young mother promptly burst into tears, and Sophie hurried around the desk to slip a comforting arm around her shoulders.

I don't think I'm supposed to hold or pat the patients any more, she thought irrationally, remembering a directive she had seen recently that spoke of medical people protecting themselves against charges of over-familiarity and sexual harassment. She continued to pat, looking down at the sleeping infant with a silly smile on her face.

'He's a beautiful baby,' she assured the young mother, her admiration warming her voice. 'Now, I know what your husband fears, but the consequences of not immunising Joel can be far more devastating. The risk of a bad reaction to immunisation is very, very slim——'

'Kent says he knows of a child who was brain-damaged following a triple antigen,' Mrs Warren explained.

'There have been extremely rare cases where a reaction has included a high fever and encephalopathy, but it has usually occurred in children with a history of seizures, or neurological damage, or a family history of neurological disease.'

Knowing she was bewildering her patient with words, Sophie retreated behind her desk once more, and picked up the woman's file.

'Are you and your husband both healthy?'

She received a watery smile and a nod.

'Have either of you ever suffered from epilepsy?'

A quick shake of the curly head answered the question.

'Do you know if you ever had febrile convulsions—small fits caused by a high temperature—when you were a child?'

'Mum says I never had a day's sickness in my life,' Mrs Warren claimed, and Sophie smiled in response to the earnest tones.

'And you had a normal, uncomplicated delivery with Joel? No delays, no problems?'

Again the woman nodded.

'Then the risk of Joel reacting badly to a triple antigen is much, much lower than the risk of his becoming seriously ill because he hasn't had one. Many parents are concerned, as you and your husband are, by the stories of risk, and as a result fewer and fewer children are being immunised.'

'But does that matter?'

'It does when you consider that seven children and a number of older people died of diptheria in a hospital not far north of here last winter,' Sophie said, the anger she felt at such needless waste undisguised in her voice. 'Diptheria is more prevalent now than at any time since early last century, when thousands of people a year died very painful and lingering deaths from the disease.'

'But what if I insist on the injection and Joel gets a bad reaction? My husband will blame me!'

Sophie nodded tiredly. It was a no-win situation! She could hardly force the woman to have the child immunised, and the husband had opted out of this visit, so, whatever happened, it would be his wife's fault!

'Why don't you bring your husband in to see me?' she suggested as calmly as her churning anger would allow. 'Then I can explain the pros and cons to him, and let him help you decide. It is only the pertussis or whooping cough vaccine that causes problems. He might opt to have the CDT vaccine against diptheria and tetanus. Joel would be at risk of whooping cough, but it would alleviate your husband's fears about possible brain damage.'

The woman brightened perceptibly, clutching her precious son even closer to her chest and smiling lovingly down on the little bald head.

'I think I'll do that. He knocks off work at about five o'clock and is usually home by five-thirty. Will you still be here then?'

'I hope not,' Sophie told her. 'I was on an early shift this morning, but I'll be starting at five again the day after tomorrow, so why not bring him in before he goes to work?'

As she ushered mother and baby out of the door, she wondered about the clinic's policy with regard to its doctors. She seemed to be telling a large number of people to come back and see *her* as distinct from 'a doctor'! Did it matter?

Sipping at the coffee Kate delivered, she decided not. Those patients who wanted to see the same doctor each time would go elsewhere if such a service were not open to them at the clinic. From that point of view, she told herself cheerfully, her eyes straying to the fallen tree beyond the window, she was positively helping the clinic in building up a regular patient base, which meant a regular flow of income.

Her thoughts twisted away from the finances of the clinic, drifting into a strange daydream where Mr Calgary Cowboy Williams was responsible for her for the rest of her life, and proving his commitment to that trust in a very physical manner!

CHAPTER FOUR

A SHIFT that began at five in the morning was supposed to end at three in the afternoon, but Sophie was still at her desk at five-thirty, checking results of tests and reports from specialists, then writing up the necessary notes on patient files.

'I know you're not officially here, but there's a Mr Williams outside who wants to see you.'

The messenger was Lucy, the newest and youngest of the reception staff, a chubby teenager who reminded Sophie of her own younger self. She quelled an urge to speak harshly to the youngster, knowing her anger had been stirred by an unaccountable fear of seeing the man yet again.

Heaven knew, he was causing enough turmoil in her thoughts already, without having him popping in and out of her rooms like a jack-in-the-box!

'I'm not on duty for patients,' she told Lucy gently. 'He'll have to see one of the other doctors.'

'Oh, he said he doesn't want to see a doctor. He wants to see you on a personal matter.'

The silly child blushed, as if she thought this was a romantic assignation, then added, 'He's ever so good-looking and I'm sure I've seen him in the papers,' in tones of unabashed awe.

It was probably to complain about the kitten, Sophie decided, cursing herself for making him responsible for the tiny orphan. Yet the thought twined through her daydream and warm blood pulsed through her body, awakening it to unfamiliar life.

Lucy stood across the desk in silence, obviously at a loss as to what to do, while the doctor to whom she had delivered her message stared helplessly out of the window. Sophie forced her mind to untangle the silly dream and think logically.

'He brought in one of his workmen earlier. He must want to see me about that. Send him in!'

The words were no sooner uttered than she felt a sharp stab of regret. If she'd added, In a few minutes, she would, firstly, have made him wait, which would have done his ego no end of good, and, secondly, been able to freshen up her lipstick and dab some powder on what was undoubtedly a very shiny nose!

The idea was so foreign to her nature that she shuddered, recognising forces at work within her that were as unfamiliar as paranormal phenomena or existentialism or Tibetan yaks!

She was Sophie—practical, down-to-earth, unromantic, unappealing to men! So why was she thinking about lipstick?

'I spoke to the council about your friends' plans!'

The words preceded him into the room, as if he wanted to say what he had to say and leave as quickly as possible.

Sophie's eyes were drawn to his face as he advanced towards her, then stood, palms resting on her desk, leaning close enough to. . .

'Kiss' was the word that sprang to mind, but that was because a tattered remnant of the daydream still hovered in her mind.

She removed her gaze almost forcibly from the well-shaped lips, sliding it upwards to see if she could detect those tiny black specks in his eyes.

'I also spoke to the architect who drew

up the plans and explained the changes he would have to make. It should all go through quite smoothly now.'

He was so close that she could see where the dark lashes sprang from his eyelids, curling upwards in a way that would make most women sigh in envy.

'Are you listening to me?'

The abrupt question slammed into her brain and she shrank back in the chair, trying vainly to recall some echo of his words.

'Are you tired? How long have you been at work?' he demanded, and she shook her head in an attempt to regain some control over the situation.

'I'm sorry, I was thinking of something else.' She smiled appeasingly up at him, but stayed where she was, pressed back in her chair, in order to put as much space as possible between them. 'You were saying something about the plans?'

'I was explaining that I had sorted out your friends' problems, but you seem to have forgotten about them. Does their building a suitable home mean so little to you now?'

He glared at her, and as she watched his

face she saw the expression shift from impatience to conjecture.

'Or was that letter simply an excuse?'

The question puzzled her and she frowned blankly at him.

'An excuse for what?'

'Don't act the innocent with me, Doctor, dear!' he sneered, a harshness in his voice that frightened her with its cold undertones.

'Don't call me that,' she snapped, angered by her own confusion.

'Well, don't play games with me, OK?' he countered, then slid his hands forward across the polished surface of her desk, so that his body loomed menacingly above her, and the shapely lips she'd avoided studying came closer and closer, until they touched hers with a fire that flared into a terrible hunger.

'I prefer women who come right out and say they are interested in me to little girls who play the innocent and use their friends' problems as an excuse to arrange a meeting.' He drew back as he spoke.

'Why, you egotistical—!'

He moved more quickly than she would have believed possible! One hand shot out to seize her flying wrist, while the other moved to cover her mouth lightly, cool against the flaming flesh. Heart thumping with an erratic reaction, she bit down into the finger that strayed too far between her sensitised lips.

'Don't say it!' he warned, pulling his hand away and raising it to his own lips to rub the tip of his tongue over the indentations left by her teeth. 'Just don't say anything!'

He flung her other hand down on to the table, like an object discarded distastefully, and turned away, as if the view beyond the window had drawn him too.

Sophie shivered, tossed once again into uncharted emotional waters by the presence and unpredictability of this man. She licked her lips, suddenly dry, mimicking the movement of his tongue on the finger that had felt so hard and cool between them only seconds earlier.

'Will you let them know?'

Was he the irrational one? She battled to make some sense of the twisting, turning conversation, now accusing, now demanding, now placatory!

'Let who know what?' she mumbled, totally bemused.

'You haven't heard a word I've said,' he

accused, leaning forward again so that his nearness cast its own spell. 'Are you finished here?'

She nodded, pleased that the motor centre of her brain still seemed to be functioning effectively.

'Then come on. I'll take you out to the site office and show you the altered plans. Maybe if I explain in words of one syllable, even a doctor will be able to understand.'

He reached out and grasped her arm, pulling her awkwardly to her feet and dragging her, stumbling slightly, behind him towards the door. It was easier to follow than to engage in a futile, public struggle, she decided, but her legs were stiff and her body unyielding, so he could not possibly get the impression that she was going with him willingly.

'I'll drive you out there and bring you back to collect your car,' he announced, steering her towards a dusty Land Cruiser parked by the kerb.

Did kidnap victims feel as bemused as this? Sophie wondered, her body moving mechanically into the front seat of the car in response to the man's orders and his firm, guiding hand.

'I don't have to see the plans,' she protested at last as he climbed into the driver's seat and fired the engine. 'If you say they will be altered to receive the necessary council approval, I believe you.'

He sat staring straight ahead, but made no move to engage the gears and pull out from the kerb. She reached out and touched his arm, uncertain in his presence, yet puzzled by a suggestion of a similar uncertainty in this man who had been so forceful in all their previous dealings.

'I didn't mean to sound as if I doubted you,' she said. Her fingers lingered on his warm, bare flesh, reluctant to move, until she remembered his suspicion of her and pulled her hand away.

'Meegan—one of the three who bought the land—is staying at the Coastside motel. I'll drive over there on my way home and tell her the good news.'

She opened the car door as she spoke, meaning to escape as quickly as she politely could, without seeming as if she was running away from him. Not that he was likely to believe that any woman would run away from him! she reminded herself. The man had an ego to suit his size!

'I'd like to show you my suggestions for the plans,' he said at last, breaking a silence that was becoming uncomfortable. 'Perhaps we could drive out to the site office then have a bite to eat somewhere before going to the motel to see your friend.'

Sophie cursed her inexperience! Why did he want her company? First he accused her of using her friends as an excuse to chase after him, and now he was the one thinking up lame excuses to keep them together. Was this the way men behaved when they were interested in a woman? The thought made her want to laugh out loud. How ridiculous to imagine that a man like Calgary Williams—who, by his own admission, had more than enough women clinging to him— would be interested in her, a plain, still slightly overweight Italian-Australian doctor with no more sex appeal than a pricked balloon!

'Well?' he demanded, and she heard the commanding tones back in his voice and relaxed. She could handle his bullying better than she could handle his uncertainty.

'I suppose I have to eat,' she muttered ungraciously. 'And if we go to the site office we could pick up the plans and show

Meegan what you are suggesting. After all, it's her house, not mine.'

'Well, shut your car door and let's get going,' he commanded, as if she'd been the one delaying things all along. 'My secretary is cat-sitting and she'll expect overtime if I'm late getting back.'

He took off, his driving as carelessly confident as his manner had been when first they'd met.

'Tell me about your friends!'

It was an order she should have resented but she found she was pleased to talk.

'I only know Meegan,' she explained. 'I met her when I was a student and doing a practical placement at a boarding-school for children with cerebral palsy. Most of the children were from country areas, sent down to the city for operations to ease contracted tendons or for blocks of intensive physiotherapy. Do you know anything about cerebral palsy?'

She turned towards him as she asked the question, and saw the casual shrug and non-committal shake of his head.

'Do you want to know?' The question was confrontational as the familiar flare of annoyance that uncaring ignorance prompted within her heated the words.

'I wouldn't have asked if I didn't,' he replied calmly, his concentration on the traffic, now building to madness at the end of the working day.

'Well, most people don't want to know,' she told him, not bothering to hide the aggression she was feeling. 'Unless people are personally touched by disability in any of its forms, their lack of knowledge is frightening. It's an almost fearful closing of the senses, as if to say, If I don't know about these things, it can't happen to me!'

With the car halted in a line of traffic at an intersection, he turned and grinned at her.

'Generalising a bit there, Doctor, dear,' he taunted, with a quirking of his lips that seemed to change the angles of his face. 'I hate to poke holes in what is obviously one of your pet theories, but unless people are personally touched by splitting the atom they don't want to know about that either!'

'That's a ridiculous analogy!' she argued. 'Atom-splitting is advanced scientific knowledge; disability is a personal issue.'

'Only if it touches you in some way, as you said earlier.' He eased the car forward in the traffic, his eyes on the road but his body sending signals that compelled her to remain alert. 'My argument is that after we leave school we choose what we want to learn about, whether it's nuclear physics or disability. If a musical note catches our fancy, we find out about the instrument that produced it, not because we have to, but because of a personal experience.'

She thought about what he was saying, certain that there must be a flaw in his argument, but unable to find it.

They left the main road, turning in at the entrance to the estate.

'It's not that people evade knowledge of disability—or atom-splitting, for that matter,' he said as he pulled up outside the small building. It's simply that they have little interest in things that don't have a personal connection.'

His hand reached down into the gap between their seats to unclip his seatbelt, and his body, twisting slightly, came closer in the encapsulating interior of the car. His last words, 'personal connection', clanged alarmingly in her mind.

'There's also the fact that people who do have specialised knowledge often find it hard to share that knowledge, Doctor, dear,' he continued in silken tones, looking down into her eyes with a strange expression on his face. 'Having come into contact with disability, I asked a question because I wished to know more. Did you answer it?'

He was so close that he seemed to absorb all the air in the confined space, so that she felt a fluttering breathlessness. She clamped her lips shut, afraid that any attempt at speech might reveal her unstable state.

Why didn't he move? Surely he wouldn't kiss her again?

The memory of those two kisses agitated her even more, and her body trembled, no longer obedient to her commands but living a life of its own. Actually excited at the prospect of a third kiss! she realised with some dismay.

'There are different forms of cerebral palsy,' she gabbled at last, forcing herself to speak in an effort to ignore the errant sensations flooding her body.

'Tell me in the office,' he murmured, his hand brushing against her thigh as he undid the clasp on her seatbelt.

The words echoed in her brain. Ordinary

words yet somehow as seductive as any of the clichés she had ever heard in films.

This is ridiculous, she told herself firmly as she followed him towards the door. You are allowing a sudden spurt of hormone activity to cloud your thinking. You are not a sixteen-year-old smitten by the first boy who ever smiled at you. You are twenty-seven years old and beyond all that kind of thing.

He had stopped in the doorway, holding the door open for her, and the smile he gave her made her forget the lecture she was delivering to herself as she battled to control knees gone suddenly wobbly.

It's inexperience, she assured herself. That's all it is! If you hadn't been so over-weight as a teenager, you'd have had a few boyfriends, gone out a bit more, and would know how to handle this silly kind of flirting.

'This is Andrea Walsh, my secretary. Andrea, meet Dr Delano, the person responsible for this!'

He held up his hand and Sophie noticed the ball of orange fur curled up in his big palm. Had he picked up the kitten the moment he walked into the office? Did that mean the tiny creature had found a weak spot in his cynically armoured heart?

She smiled at Andrea, who was saying hello and goodbye, gathering up her handbag and some shopping bags as she prepared to leave work for the day.

Sophie saw her disappear out of the door with a feeling of regret. She was now alone with this man who was disrupting her peaceful existence—as alone as a solitary explorer pushing deeper and deeper into unmapped territory.

'So tell me about your friend and her own particular form of cerebral palsy,' he ordered, perching on the edge of the desk and pushing the swivelling office chair towards her with a negligent foot.

'Meegan has ataxic CP, which is caused by damage to the cerebellum, here at the base of the brain near the brain stem.' She pushed her fingers into the short hair at the nape of her neck to illustrate the point. 'It means she has problems with balance and co-ordination. Her speech is also affected, but she is able to make herself understood.'

She slumped into the chair as she spoke, then wished she'd remained standing. She was following the man's orders too willingly!

'Is she one of the two in a wheelchair?'

The questions surprised her, until she remembered explaining about the nuisance value of hallways.

'She has an electric wheelchair she uses most of the time, but can walk short distances with sticks, and support herself for long enough to be self-sufficient in her personal care needs.'

'You mean she can bath herself!'

It was a statement, not a question, but it made Sophie remember her vow to avoid the dreadful jargon that developed in social welfare fields. She'd fallen into the habit again—and in front of this man who seemed determined to find fault with everything she said or did.

'And the other two?'

Was he really interested? she wondered, then answered anyway. Better to keep talking than have time to think!

'One is a young man who became a paraplegic following an accident. Meegan has met him recently and is. . .has. . .'

'Fallen in love, perhaps?'

Sophie felt the blush rising from her toes.

'She's interested in him,' she said stiffly.

'Does her disability preclude it being

love?' he probed, and her embarrassment deepened. 'Aren't you being as prejudiced as you accused me of being yesterday, by denying the girl normal feelings?'

'I am not denying her normal feelings,' she argued, but part of her mind remembered Meegan's blush and wondered. 'How would I know if she's in love or not?'

'You're her friend,' he pointed out logically, depositing the kitten back into the box on the desk beside him. 'Surely she would tell you, pour out her feelings, share the joy, et cetera, et cetera? Isn't that what women do?'

'I wouldn't know!' she said coldly, forcing herself to respond casually to his taunts.

'No, Doctor, darling? It's not because you're not a woman.' His eyes slid over her in a blatantly obvious assessment of her well-concealed shape. 'So is it that you've never been in love?'

His voice was like a snake, slithering into dark corners of her mind, and filling her with a nameless fear.

'No, I haven't,' she said stoutly, trying to fight the unseen menace with common sense. 'And if being in love entails sharing girlish confidences with my friends, then I'm thankful I haven't had the experience.'

'Never been in love? I don't believe you! Never felt your pulse race as you picked up the telephone, expecting to hear his voice? Never felt your heart flip over when you glimpsed someone who looked like him in the street? Never felt sweat break out on the palms of your hands as he passed by?'

He paused, looking down at her with the intent, disbelieving expression of a scientist studying a new, and most unusual specimen. She hoped he couldn't see any hint of her dismay as he described, so accurately, the sensations that his unwelcome presence in her life had been causing.

'It's a physical reaction,' he said slowly. 'It happens involuntarily. It isn't something you choose, but something that chooses you. Have you really escaped its clutches or do you deny it because your neat, scientific mind can't explain it?'

She shrugged, hoping to convey an impression of nonchalance, although his words were plunging deep into her heart, hurting her with their sarcastic condemnation.

'I don't know if Meegan is in love with

Mark, only that they became sufficiently friendly to decide they would like to share a house. Gerald is a friend of Mark's, and by including him they scraped together enough money to pay for the land and build the house,' she said flatly, meeting his disbelieving stare with a defiant frown. 'And whether love enters into it is neither my business nor yours, Mr Williams.'

'Whether love exists at all is more the question you need answered,' he remarked cryptically. 'Now, where shall we eat? Do you like Thai food?'

Drowning must feel like this, Sophie decided as she tried to follow the contrary currents of his conversation.

'I don't think I want to eat with you after all,' she mumbled feebly. 'If I could just have a look at the plan, so I can explain the changes to Meegan——'

'Breaking our first date?'

His grey eyes caught and held hers, and she suspected that the glimmer she saw in their depths was amusement—at her expense!

'It's hardly a date!'

'Are you certain of that?' he probed, and again the warmth that his suggestive tone could generate so easily flooded through her.

'Of course it isn't,' she told him repressively, at the same time trying to use will-power to cool her over-heating blood. 'A date implies an interest in each other. All we were talking about was eating together, and I've changed my mind about that.'

'Why?'

No probing now, just one hard word!

'Because I'm tired of being the butt of your weird sense of humour!' she said tartly. 'It may amuse you to mock me as you're doing, but it's not as funny from this end!'

'Why would it amuse me to make fun of you?' he demanded, the deep voice filling with anger. 'What makes you think I'm mocking you?'

'What makes me think——?' Her own anger rose to meet and match his. 'Isn't calling me "Doctor, dear" in that sneering voice a mockery? Isn't all that talk about love, and poking and prodding at me about it, just a little diversion for your own amusement? The great lover of Westport, amusing himself at the expense of the dumpy little doctor.'

She blinked back the tears that burned as bitter as acid behind her eyelids, projecting all the pain and hurt that her appearance had caused over the years into a blinding glare of rage.

'Is that how you see yourself?' he demanded, straightening up as if her attack had been physical. 'A dumpy little doctor? Where's your self-esteem, your feelings of self-worth? You dare to characterise yourself that way, then blame me for mocking you?'

'Well, I am a dumpy little doctor,' she told him defensively. 'But I'm a good doctor and there's more to people than their looks.'

He leaned forward towards her, speaking slowly and carefully.

'You're the one who introduced looks into the conversation.'

Then, suddenly, there were no words left, and no anger building to fuel a fight. Sophie slumped deeper into the chair, her eyes fixed on his face, trying to see beyond the taut skin and hard-angled bone, trying to probe the workings of his mind and find if there was any meaning, any feeling, even, behind the words that flowed so easily.

'Given up the argument?' he contended, almost gently, then turned away, without waiting for a response, to shuffle through papers on a bench. 'We'll take the plans; you can look at them over dinner. Did you say Thai food would do?'

She sighed and nodded. There was obviously no point in arguing with the man. He pretended to take in what she said, but continued inexorably on his way regardless, so she might just as well keep her mouth shut. Did they call him The Cowboy because he rode over objections, excuses, protests and denials with such ease—sweeping everything and everyone up on the way?

She watched him tidy up a desk, sorting through small message slips with an intentness she found fascinating. His fingers picked up and discarded the slips in turn, moving with an elegance she would not have imagined in such a big man.

'I hope you're not a sulker!' he remarked, glancing across at her silent form.

She shook her head, unable to explain that, now the urge to fight him had slipped away, she found his presence soothing. It must be something to do with watching someone else work, she decided as the tension slid out of her body.

'All done,' he said at last, tucking a roll of plans under his arm and picking up the box that held the sleeping kitten.

'Do you really have to take it wherever you go?' she asked, horrified that she should have caused him so much trouble.

'Well, I did leave it in the office when I visited you earlier,' he confessed with a grin, 'and Andrea offered to take it home with her, but I thought maybe your friend Meegan would like to meet it. After all, a new house needs a cat to make it homely.'

He was watching her with an expectant look on his face, and Sophie shook her head and chuckled.

'I think it's a wonderful idea, but I might have known you'd slide out of the responsibility somehow!'

'Snap judgement, Doctor, dear?'

One dark eyebrow cocked, but a trace of his earlier good humour still softened his features.

'Maybe an erroneous assumption based on your celebrated lifestyle,' she admitted, taking the bite out of the words with a rueful smile. It would be a shame to spoil the ease that had settled between them with another argument!

She stood up and stretched, feeling tireder now that she had relaxed.

'A quick meal, a visit to your friend, then an early night for you,' he said briskly, hustling her towards the door. 'Do you often work that early shift?'

'Three days a week,' she told him as they walked out into the darkening tranquillity of the tree-littered estate, 'but the latest I work is midnight. I don't ever work the awful ten p.m. to six a.m. shift.'

'I bet the doctors who do work it are out of the place by six-ten,' he muttered, opening the car door for her and guiding her up into the high seat, 'not there two hours after they've supposed to have finished, like you were today!'

'I don't like to leave things not done,' she explained, trying to sound quite calm and composed although his hand, warm and firm beneath her elbow, was causing more of the symptoms he'd described earlier.

Such physical manifestations must be the result of a chemical attraction, she told herself firmly as he reached up and pulled the seatbelt down, pressing the clasp into her hand. She wished she'd thought of that earlier. She could have argued that accelerated heartbeats didn't equate with love, but sexual chemistry.

The thought made her blush in the darkness, and she was glad he'd shut the door and was walking around the front of the car. If he'd been any closer, he'd have sensed her agitation.

Thank heavens she hadn't thought of it earlier and blurted it out, she realised as he climbed into the car beside her and deposited the kitten's box in her lap. The very thought of arguing about sexuality with this man was enough to tie her tongue in knots for days!

An easy silence settled between them as they drove through the quiet streets of his estate towards the main road. A solid line of cars greeted them, the headlights trailing through the darkness like an abandoned string of party lights.

'There must be an accident up ahead somewhere,' she remarked, feeling the tightening of her stomach muscles that had become familiar when she'd worked in the accident and emergency department of the hospital.

'Do you have to get involved?' he asked quietly.

'Not have to,' she told him, nodding at the same time as instinct and training combined as they had only yesterday, and urged her to hurry to the scene to offer services that might otherwise be too late.

'I'll drive down along here,' he replied calmly, steering the big vehicle over the rutted verge and along the nature strip beside the road. 'There are no creeks or gullies for us to fall into,' he added, with a conspiratorial smile.

'You're enjoying this!' she accused, feeling his pulsing excitement.

'Of course I am,' he acknowledged. 'What red-blooded male doesn't enjoy a challenge, a chance to be a hero in a woman's eyes——?'

He broke off to concentrate on steering the car adroitly through a gutter deep enough to be called a gully, laughing triumphantly as he pulled out the other side.

'Most woman equate heroism with stupidity!' Sophie told him tartly, shaken by the fear that had gripped her as they had plunged into the dark hole.

'There's a thin line!' he agreed so equably

that she peered suspiciously at his face in the dim light reflecting from the road.

Flashing lights told her they had reached the accident, and she was relieved to see an ambulance, as well as the usual clutter of police cars. Her chauffeur pulled up, well clear of the service vehicles, then lifted the kitten in its box on to the back seat.

'I'll help you up on to the road,' he told her as she prepared to slip out of the car. 'It's rough ground and a doctor with a broken leg won't be able to help anyone.'

She was glad of his support as she stumbled up the slope to the tarred surface. Her eyes took in the scene and she felt a wash of gladness sweep over her as she realised that the accident had been a minor one. Although four cars showed signs of damage, they were superficial dents and concertinaed metal, not the horrific scene that her over-active imagination had envisaged.

'A few aches and pains but no serious injuries,' a policeman told her when she introduced herself. 'One car was attempting to overtake, then pulled back into the line of traffic when the driver realised it wasn't safe. Caused end-to-end damage, which is always better than a head-on.'

'How involved would you have got if it had been a bad accident?'

The question came out of the darkness as they drove on towards the town.

'I'd have done whatever was necessary and possible,' she told him, wondering where the conversation was leading.

'Bandaged wounds, stopped bleeding, that sort of stuff?'

'Of course, but it's only basic first aid. Anyone would do the same.'

'Would they?' he asked, the cynicism she disliked in him back in his voice. 'I don't think so, Doctor, dear. Not these days! But you would have rushed in there, with no bag, so no gloves, ignoring the risk of contamination, and you talk about heroism and stupidity!'

'You drove me down there knowing I had no bag,' she argued, annoyed that he had forced her to defend herself again, but unwilling to admit the element of truth in his words.

'Ah, but I'm a man!' he countered triumphantly.

As if I didn't know! she thought as she bit her tongue, refusing to carry the silly conversation any further in case she betrayed more and more of her essentially private self to this prying egomaniac.

CHAPTER FIVE

'IT'S A funny little lump,' Mrs Wentworth was saying, fingering her neck, as Sophie dragged her mind back to the present and tried to concentrate on her patient. She had always been so focused on her work that the moments of abstraction she was suffering today bothered her. Her brain seemed to be working on two planes, so that consciously she was considering her patient's problem while subconsciously her mind replayed snippets of last night's date that wasn't a date.

'That's where your thyroid gland is,' she explained carefully. 'Nodules often form there—about four per cent of the population have them—and they are more common in women than in men.' She smiled reassuringly as she added, 'The good news is that eighty-five per cent are benign.'

Concentrating now, she studied the sketchy details on Mrs Wentworth's chart, thinking again that one of the problems of

working in a new clinic was that patients
had no history.

'Do you remember having thyroid problems as a child, or any other problem that
required low-dose radium treatment to your
head or neck?'

The woman shook her head.

'I'll have to feel it,' Sophie explained,
leaving her desk to stand behind her
patient. 'When did you first notice it?'

She slid her hands around the woman's
neck, letting her fingers carry out their own
tactile exploration, relying on their skill to
transmit their findings directly to her brain.

'I've had it for a while,' the woman confessed, 'but I haven't been sick and it's not
sore, so I didn't bother about it. Then you
see all these ads on the TV about cancer,
and my husband said I'd better have it
checked out.'

'If you've had it for some time and it
hasn't produced any noticeable growth,
that's a good sign,' Sophie assured her, her
fingers finding the tracheal rings at the top
of the neck, and sliding down to find the
isthmus of the thyroid crossing the second
ring. The slight, gelatinous-feeling ridge
beneath the skin told her she had found the

gland, and, with her fingers now super-
sensitive to any irregularity, she palpated
the area, finding the definitive nodule and
testing its rubbery texture.

'I'm going to feel the rest of your neck
for any signs of swelling in the lymph
glands,' she told her patient, letting her
fingers make their way to the sites she knew
could provide warnings that a carcinoma
was present.

There was no swollen lymph node in the
midline above the isthmus, and she felt a
small thrill of relief, as a malignancy of the
size of this nodule would be affecting the
lymph system by now.

Her hands traced the lymph drainage
through the neck area, then she felt the
nodule once again before returning to her
chair to note her findings on the file and
sketch in the position of the small lump.

'All the signs say that it is benign,' she
said, 'but it's best to be certain. I can aspirate the nodule, which means inserting a
needle and removing a sample of the epi-
thelial cells. We have these tested for a
definite diagnosis. If it is a cyst, the aspir-
ation could make it disappear, although it
doesn't always get rid of it for good. If it

refills, we can aspirate it again, or remove it surgically.'

'Should I have it done straight away?'

'Is someone with you?' Sophie asked, knowing that the procedure would be painful and could leave Mrs Wentworth feeling uncomfortable.

'Not today, but my husband's not working at the moment, so he could come back with me another time.'

'That would be best. In the meantime, I'll order a series of blood and urine tests that will show if your thyroid is functioning normally.'

She pulled a medical laboratory form towards her and began to designate the tests she wanted carried out. If she started with serum T_4 and T_3 test and a serum cholesterol count, then higher levels of thyroxine and lowered cholesterol would indicate hyperthyroidism. She thought for a moment, then decided to add Resin Triiodothyronine uptake and free T_4 index tests as neither of these required special preparation. If any of the tests showed cause for alarm, she would order further tests.

'Sometimes a nodule like that will take on the activity of the thyroid gland and actually secrete thyroid hormone, which will lead to an increase in the level in the blood, and what we call hyperthyroidism,' she explained.

Her eyes looked up to scan the patient again, although her preliminary examination had shown none of the obvious signs. Mrs Wentworth's hair was thick and glossy, her eyes bright, but not protuberant, and her skin looked clear and dry. No tell-tale red patches marked her elbows, and there was no manifestation of nervous tension or restlessness in her patient.

Could there be hypothyroidism? she wondered, then stopped the conjecture, knowing that the tests would tell her if there was any problem with the gland's functioning.

'Hyperthyroidism and hypothyroidism caused by an underactive thyroid can both be treated,' she continued, 'so there's no need to be concerned about it. Here's the form to take to the medical laboratory next door. I'll come out to the desk with you to make your next appointment. I want to organise a time when another doctor can assist.'

She led the way towards the door, hoping

she didn't sound too tentative. She had seen illustrations of how to aspirate thyroid nodules, and had probably practised it on the teaching dolls during her training, but, although she had tried to sound confident, she knew she'd prefer to assist this first time.

'You could have sent her on to an endocrine specialist,' Dr Crane, her senior colleague, told her gruffly when she explained the problem to him.

'But it's a normal general practice procedure,' she argued. 'Or was, until this fad for referring everything possible came into vogue. Patients go from us to a specialist then back to us, where we read a scientific explanation of the problem and translate it for the patient. It's too impersonal.'

'So you really believe in the old-fashioned values of general practice?'

Sophie nodded vigorously.

'I think people like to know their doctor. They like to be able to ring him and say, This is happening to me now; what does it mean? They can't ring a specialist after he's aspirated their thyroid—specialists are far too busy! And after a referral their local doctor doesn't know enough about what the specialist has done to answer their question correctly. The patients are caught in a vacuum.'

'Radical thinking for one so young,' Dr Crane remarked with a smile. 'I'll be happy to aspirate your thyroid for you this time, then be your assistant when the next one crops up. With someone like you in this clinic, we might just manage to turn it from a twenty-four-hour convenience for people whose GPs are not available into a genuine family practice.'

'Wouldn't that be great?' Sophie responded, smiling broadly at the hidden compliment, before hurrying back to her room to tackle the next problem of the day.

If the clinic became more practice-orientated, she could stay on, and these people she was seeing day by day would become her regular patients. The thought diverted her from her earlier distraction, when the memories of 'call me Cal' Williams and the strange evening they had spent together had floated persistently across the surface of her mind.

She heard the screaming child before she reached her door, and turned to see an anxious mother carrying the distraught toddler through the front entrance of the clinic, followed by a man with the palm of his hand pressed to his mouth.

Sensing an emergency, she moved to meet the little family, ushering them straight past the waiting patients and into her room.

'What's happened?' she asked the mother, who was trying to stem the noise by jigging the little boy up and down on her hip.

'He was in the garden, playing near the little covered fish-pond we've got there, and then he came running in, screaming like this and holding his mouth. We thought it must be poison at first—a dog bait or something out of a cupboard—but we couldn't find anything at all. He'd been chopping at some plants—elephant's ears—you know, the ones with the big leaves—and I think he must have got a bit on his fingers, then brushed them on his mouth.'

While his mother explained, Sophie turned the child so that she could look into his mouth as he dragged in more air to cry again. There was no swelling of his tongue, nor exceptional redness on his lips. She pressed the buzzer on her desk, and, when Kate appeared in response, asked her to bring in some milk, a baby's bottle and a glass.

'Will he still take a bottle?' she asked the mother, and was pleased to see her nod of assent.

'I tried him with some juice when he first started screaming,' she said, 'but he wouldn't drink it.'

'Juice could have exacerbated the tender spots but milk should neutralise the effects of the poison,' Sophie explained. 'It will also soothe the affected tissues, although it won't heal any areas that contact with the sap has actually burnt. It's like a heat burn on your skin—nothing will make it better straight away, although the surface areas in the mouth heal more rapidly than the outer skin of your body.'

Kate returned with a tray of most unmedical-like equipment, and Sophie filled the bottle and handed it to the mother, who sat down, cradling the little blond boy and talking soothingly to him while she persuaded him to take the milk.

'Kate, would you please phone the poisons centre and ask for any information they might have on a plant commonly known as elephant's-ears?'

'It has big green leaves with heavy veining in purplish tones,' the woman added, relaxing now that the child was drinking the milk.

As the noise subsided to hiccuping sobs, Sophie turned to the father, still standing by the door, his hand across his mouth.

'You too?' she asked, seeing the pain on his face.

'He refused to believe that anything in the garden could upset Jamie like this, so he picked up a bit of the cut-off plant and chewed it.' Disbelief tinged the woman's explanation.

The man appeared to be breathing normally, Sophie decided, ushering him towards her second chair, and automatically beginning the procedure of taking his blood-pressure and pulse.

Satisfied that he was not suffering any unobservable side-effects, she sought visual signs of damage.

'Did you swallow it?' she asked, prising away his fingers to peer inside his mouth, noting immediately the grotesquely swollen lips.

He shook his head, and his wife continued the explanation.

'He felt it burning on his tongue and spat it out.'

'Just as well,' Sophie said, shaking her head as she thought of possible consequences. 'There's some swelling of your tongue already. Swallowing it could have caused sufficient swelling in the oesophagus to close off your trachea, and we'd have had to operate to allow you to breathe.'

The man went paler, and shook his head again.

'As it is,' Sophie continued, 'I'd like you to stay here for an hour. I'll put you in a private room and delegate one of the nurses to watch for any signs of difficulty in breathing. If even a tiny bit trickled into your throat, you could have a severe reaction. In the meantime, I guess you're wanting to scream just as loudly as your son was?'

The man nodded, and Sophie passed him a glass of milk.

'Drink this, and keep drinking. I'll get the nurse to make up an ice-pack you can slide around inside your mouth and hold between your lips to help ease the pain, but I can't give you any pain-killers just yet. They could mask any further reaction you might have.'

Her patient groaned, but Sophie was adamant. A grown man stupid enough to chew on an unknown substance would just have to suffer for his actions!

'Come on,' she said cheerfully, 'I'll show you a room where you can wait in comfort, and find a nurse to monitor both the patients.'

As Jamie was now quiet, she was inclined to believe the mother's supposition that he had rubbed a small amount of sap from the plant on to either his lips or tongue. The milk had neutralised the action sufficiently to take away the pain.

The father was a different problem. Because he had chewed the noxious substance, saliva would have carried particles of it throughout his mouth, and he would suffer all the usual symptoms of burning, including exceedingly painful blisters that were likely to take a week or more to heal.

She led the way through to one of the small procedure-rooms, and adjusted one end of the couch so that it became a recliner. She waved the father on to it, then went out and brought in a light, tubular plastic armchair for the mother and child.

'Sally will be in with more milk, and I'll

come and check you in half an hour or so,' she told them as they settled down to wait.

Kate handed her the information from the poisons centre as she walked back through the busy waiting-room, and it confirmed Sophie's own deduction that the toxin was fast-acting, and locally effective, but, unless swallowed, causing irritation and inflammation of the oesophagus and lining of the stomach, it would not promote any secondary symptoms like anaphylactic shock, muscle spasms or heart failure.

'Ask Sally to go into room three and keep an eye on both the father and the son,' she said quietly to Kate. 'They'll need more milk and she could take their details for new files while she's in there. I'll add my observations and suggestions later.'

Kate slipped away to find Sally, one of the three nurses usually on duty in the clinic, while Sophie walked over to her door and picked up the patient file awaiting her in the box.

'Mr Ambrose!'

A quick glance round the waiting-room found yesterday's patient, back as ordered for her to check on his hand. Was it her insistence or his boss's command that had brought him here?

She showed him through to her room, apologising for the delay.

'I could hear you had a more urgent problem,' the man reassured her with a smile. 'Kid all right, is he?'

'I think so,' Sophie told him, explaining how easy it was for children to be harmed by seemingly innocent plants or substances around their homes.

'Forty children could have played in that garden and not chopped into those plants,' she told him, 'but until you get the one who does you have no idea that those decorative leaves are potentially fatal.'

'I've got a book on poisonous garden plants, and I took out all the ones in my garden, even things like rubber trees, because the sap can blind you.'

'It's a good idea,' Sophie agreed, 'especially if you have children. Now, how's the hand?'

'A bit stiff and sore,' David Ambrose admitted as Sophie removed the light bandage she had put in place the day before.

'There's infection present.' She sighed as

she saw the angry colour. 'I'm going to bathe it again, then apply some antibiotic powder. A topical application might help fight whatever strange bacteria you've got in there.'

She washed away the seeping moisture, then snipped débrided scraps of tissue from the edge of the wound, before puffing powder all over the surface.

'I'll wrap it again. A penicillin injection would boost the antibiotics you're already taking. . .'

She offered the suggestion hesitantly, having seen the man's reaction to the local anaesthetic and the tetanus jab she'd given him the day before.

'I'd rather give the ones I'm taking another day to work,' he protested immediately. 'It's not that sore!'

The dilemma prickled in her mind. Her instinct told her to go all out in fighting the infection, to prevent permanent damage to the hand, yet the man had a right to choose his treatment.

'Come back tonight and see whoever is on duty if it becomes more painful,' she adjured him. 'And I want to see you again in the morning—bright and early, OK?'

'OK!' the man agreed reluctantly as she re-wrapped his hand loosely. 'I know it's bad. I won't be stupid about it.' There was a slight pause before he added, 'You'd tell my boss on me if I was,' in a teasing kind of manner that brought Sophie up short.

She barely knew Cal Williams, yet something in this man's words made it seem as if they shared a particular friendship. Or was she imagining things? Had she become super-sensitive about the man?

The thoughts made her goodbye a little abrupt, and left her feeling dissatisfied and uneasy once again.

Even as a teenager, when all her friends had begun going out with boys, she had been able to lose herself completely in either study or work, blotting out the odd moments of envy with her determination to succeed. Surely she could still do that?

All she had to do was block out the images of his lean, handsome face that flitted across her mind like the intermittent flickering of a slide-show. And close her ears to the remembered cadence of his voice, low and deep, or lightened by a teasing warmth. She'd only met the man four times! So why was the impression he'd left on her senses so indelible? And why had eating with him been such a pleasure? Such fun? Had he set himself to entertain her, deliberately using his over-abundant charm to ensure that the few hours remained lodged in her memory?

'There are no signs of either of your patients' conditions deteriorating,' Sally rang through to tell her as she sat at her desk and tried to concentrate on work matters. 'The little fellow has gone off to sleep, and the father says his mouth is still very painful, but the swelling of his tongue and lips has reduced by almost half.'

'Send him back in here and I'll prescribe some pain-killers and a soothing local anaesthetic for his mouth. His wife can wait there for him, if the baby is asleep in her arms.'

'The skin inside your mouth is sore because it's burned,' she explained, when he came back into the room and dropped into a chair, a glass of milk still firmly held in his right hand.

She examined his mouth, noting the redness of the soft tissue inside his lips and across the roof of his mouth and the still angry colour of his tongue.

'At the moment the tissues are swollen,

but later that swelling will turn to blisters. Any of the proprietary lotions or paints or lozenges might help ease the pain, but SM33 Adult Formula Liquid is probably the most effective, as it will promote healing and at the same time provide a numbing effect. You paint it on the damaged areas every three hours.'

Returning to her desk, she wrote the name of the medication on a pad, then turned to him again.

'Are you allergic to anything?'

'Not that I know of!'

'Then I'll give you a script for some Panadeine Forte.' She scribbled on the script pad. 'They are a strong pain-killer, and should help you get over the next few days while the pain is at its worst. Take them only as directed, drink plenty of fluids and try to rest as much as possible. Your body has had a severe shock, and needs time to recover.'

There was a muttered, 'Thank you,' but Sophie shook her head, knowing that there was nothing more she could do, and that the man was going to have to endure several days of pain and misery before his mouth began to heal. Unfortunately, there was no magic wand she could wave to make him instantly better.

Two more patient files were waiting for her, but as she slid the first of these out of the box Kate came towards her with a message slip.

'This woman phoned and asked if you could call her back when you have a spare moment.'

She handed Sophie the piece of yellow paper with Meegan's name and the motel phone number written on it.

'That will probably be at five o'clock this afternoon,' she told Kate with a wry grin, glancing around the occupied chairs in the waiting-room.

'Oh, no, that would be too late,' the receptionist replied, and Sophie looked at her in surprise.

'Well, I asked her if it was urgent and she said that she wants to ask you to dinner,' Kate explained. 'It seems she's got cooking facilities in her motel unit and there's someone coming that she wants you to meet and she needs to know so she can do some shopping.'

It must be Mark, Sophie thought. How great!

'Could you ring her back and tell her I'm too busy to phone right now, but I would love to come? And please ask what time would suit her.'

Kate nodded, and Sophie reached out to touch her shoulder and murmur a warm, 'Thank you,' before calling her next patient and ushering the young woman into her room.

Her patients were predominately female, she realised as she greeted Nancy Davidson. Was it because women preferred to see another woman about their problems and asked for her, or because the men who attended the clinic were avoiding her, so that the women patients were steered her way?

Men and women and Meegan's call!

Activated by such minor clues, memories of the previous night beckoned her thoughts away from work once more. She had dined out in the past with associates, and with groups of friends—even, once or twice, with men she had thought might be showing an interest in her—yet last night's experience had been totally different.

Something had hummed in the air between them that was unlike anything she had ever known. It had generated its own exquisite tension, clothing ordinary words and trite politenesses in a special radiance, so that the conversation, in her memory, shimmered like a scattering of jewels, flung across her mind.

She forced herself to concentrate on her new patient, reading quickly through the file in her hand to banish another image of Cal Williams, totally at ease in Meegan's company, and laughing with her about the ridiculous notion of out-of-control electric wheelchairs hurtling off the deck of their projected pole house, into the scrub beneath.

'Please sit here and tell me what I can do for you, Miss Davidson,' she said with a warmer than usual smile as she deliberately pushed the insistent distractions to the back of her mind.

Her patient responded with a shy smile of her own, then rushed into speech.

'I know it's probably nothing to worry about, and I'm sorry to be taking up your time, but I'm getting a runny nose, and itchy eyes and sneezes every morning. I assume it's an allergy, but I'm an asthmatic and because of that I've recently shifted into a new flat with tiles instead of carpet, and absolutely nothing in the furnishings that could precipitate an attack.'

'What about plants? Is there something flowering in the garden that could be producing a pollen sensitivity?'

Her patient thought for a moment, then shook her head.

'The garden is laid out to suit the block of flats, which has that latest Mexican sort of look, so there are cacti and other succulents, lots of gravel, and a few pandanus palms—not a thing that flowers, in fact.'

'And the flat itself? If it's new, then maybe you're reacting to something in the paint, or the chemicals used to clean the place when the building was completed. As an example, many builders use an acid wash to clean newly laid tiles. There could be residual traces of the acid in your flat.'

Again there was a denying head-shake.

'I was in the place for six weeks before this started, so it can't be that. I've also cut out all the worst kind of chemical cleaners, and use only bicarbonate of soda and vinegar for cleaning, and non-allergenic soap and make-up.'

'You have gone into it thoroughly,'

Sophie said, smiling at the earnest young woman who was so determined to overcome her problems in a sensible manner.

'I had to,' Miss Davidson responded. 'I saw my mother taking all kinds of prescribed and non-prescribed remedies for her asthma and hay fever, and I'm certain they did more harm than good. The more she took, the more she seemed to need, and in the end an asthma attack killed her at the age of forty-nine.'

'I'm sorry to hear that, but at least you were made aware of the dangers,' Sophie agreed, liking this new patient more and more as she listened to her sensible conversation.

'That's why I chose this flat, and have been working so hard on controlling my allergic reactions by eliminating possible causes rather than taking something to stop it once it starts.'

'Is there something you can take to stop it?' Sophie jotted down the possible allergenics already eliminated as she listened, then paused for the name of the antihistamine.

'I take Teldane, which is terrific for the hay fever, but I don't want to be on one of those a day for the rest of my life.'

Sophie agreed, racking her brain to think of other factors that could be triggering the attacks.

'Once you've ruled out environment, there's only food,' she said. 'Have you changed your eating habits? Are you having something before you go to bed, or a different breakfast that might be causing it?'

There was a silence while her patient thought about food.

'It would have to be breakfast, because it doesn't start until after I'm up and about.'

'Well, what do you have for breakfast?'

As she asked the question, her control slipped, and into her mind flashed a similar question, though why she should be wondering what Cal Williams had for breakfast she could not fathom!

'Cereal, fruit juice, sometimes a cup of coffee, and toast.'

'It sounds innocuous enough,' Sophie told her, then remembered something she'd read in a medical magazine within the last few weeks.

'What kind of breakfast cereal?' she asked abruptly, and saw the surprise on the woman's face.

'It's one of those healthy ones, with bran and fruit and things——'

'High in fibre?' Sophie interrupted.

'Yes, it is.'

'And have you always eaten it?' Sophie persisted, and was pleased to see the dawning recognition on the woman's face.

'No,' she said slowly. 'I've only recently changed to it. Surely I couldn't be allergic to a breakfast cereal?'

'It may have an additive in it called psyllium, which is a water-soluble fibre currently being used to boost the fibre levels in cereals. It's also found in some laxatives and over-the-counter diet products. Recent tests have found that psyllium can produce allergic reactions in people with a history of allergy, hay fever or asthma.'

'I'll go straight home and read the packet,' the relieved patient announced, standing up and reaching out to shake Sophie's hand. 'Thanks for the thought!' She smiled at Sophie, who responded with a grin.

'You're the second patient in two days I've spoken to about food triggering allergic reactions. If I'm not careful I'll be changing the eating patterns of the area.'

'Wouldn't do any harm! I'm a teacher and when I see the rubbish some of the kids eat it horrifies me. Maybe, if you're going to stay in Westport, I can arrange for you to come and speak at the school from time to time. You could cover diet, cleanliness, exercise, all those kind of things, talking about them from a good health point of view! The kids seem to respond better to people they consider are experts.'

'I'd enjoy that,' Sophie told her. 'And I am staying,' she added, although as she said the words she wondered. If thoughts of the town's favourite son and most noted womaniser kept disrupting her work, then maybe moving on to somewhere else would be the only cure!

She walked to the door with Miss Davidson, the familiar surge of triumph that her possible diagnosis had brought now dimmed slightly by her inescapable thoughts, and the niggling suspicions that her common sense kept alive.

Why had Cal Williams gone out of his way to charm her? And why had he been so attentive to Meegan, sitting close to her, teasing her and making her laugh, until Sophie had felt a strange twinge of pain, although the sight of Meegan's pale face enhanced to bright prettiness by the attention should have brought her joy?

She called out the name of her next patient, bewilderment turning to anger as she realised how much this one man had disrupted the calm waters of her life. And right now, when she needed all her faculties functioning perfectly to prove herself as a general practitioner!

She remembered how she had felt as they'd travelled back to the clinic after visiting Meegan to show her the house plans. He had driven in silence through streets that had seemed unnaturally quiet. She had held her breath, not knowing what he was likely to do next, as the car had pulled up beside hers in the dark, underground car park.

Tense anticipation had screwed her nerves to straining point as she'd opened the door, then he had said, 'See you around sometime!' in a cool, ultra-casual voice, and she'd felt an overpowering urge to cry, or maybe hit him!

CHAPTER SIX

HURRYING down to her car at six, Sophie was glad that Meegan had made seven o'clock the time for dinner. Although she remembered all the warnings from lecturers about the dangers of over-working, especially during the time it took to become established in a practice, the rules of efficient time management kept slipping by her as she struggled to tie up all the loose ends of each day before she left work.

At least she had enough time to go back to her flat, shower and change before driving over to the motel.

Change into what? she wondered as she negotiated the winding streets, filled with children skate-boarding or riding push-bikes, watchful parents and chatting neighbours as people relaxed at the end of the working day.

Most of her going-out clothes were several sizes too big for her now, and, although she had bought a few skirts and blouses to

146

wear to work, she hadn't bothered to buy anything special.

'Probably because I still have visions of that ultimate shape,' she told herself, glancing ruefully down at the over-abundant curves that still denied her the illusory goal of slim and willowy.

She was late arriving at the motel, having tried on and discarded most of the items in her wardrobe. With Meegan cooking a special dinner to introduce Mark, the least she could do was dress for the occasion.

As she parked her car in the visitors' space outside the motel, she wondered if she had overdone it. The full-skirted black silk dress had always been a favourite, and she had been unwilling, or unable, to throw it out. With the broad silver belt her mother had given her last birthday clinched around her waist, it looked very festive, but maybe. . .

'You look fantastic!' Meegan greeted her, allaying her doubts.

'I was worried I might have overdone it, but you look pretty special yourself,' Sophie replied, bending to kiss her cheek.

It was true! The dark blue of Meegan's dress enhanced the clear azure of her eyes, and excitement had added a warm colour to her cheeks, giving her a look of attractive fragility, like a very special porcelain doll. Even her hair seemed to shine with a special lustre, as if something had washed her in a delicate radiance.

'Flowers for my hostess,' she added, handing over the bunch of daisies she had stopped and bought on the way.

'Come on in.' Meegan took the flowers then turned her chair and led the way into the main area of the motel room.

Sophie whistled appreciatively, noting the divan bed pushed back against the wall and the table, beautifully set and decorated with more flowers, taking pride of place in the centre.

'The manager helped me,' Meegan explained. 'Mark and Gerald are staying here as well—in the next unit, in fact— as this is one of the few motels in the area that is completely accessible for wheelchairs. Look.'

She opened the bathroom door to show Sophie the unusual layout, with the shower head poised above a grate in the floor, no constricting screen or tangling curtains, and the floor sloping imperceptibly towards the grate to do away with the need for a hob. The vanity unit had also been specially constructed, and placed slightly lower than usual. There were no drawers or cupboards beneath it, so a person in a wheelchair could glide in underneath and reach the taps or lean over the basin without impossible contortions.

'Even the door-handles and light switches have been chosen to make things easy for you,' Sophie confirmed, looking around at the special details the builders had included.

'Yes,' Meegan agreed, waving her fingers at the movement-sensitive switch. 'It's good that the motel is so modern and so close to our land, as it means we can bring our builder down here and show him what we need, instead of trying to explain.'

Sophie nodded. She had been involved with Meegan when she'd renovated a small flat for another couple who were in wheelchairs, and the problems had, at times, seemed insurmountable. To have been able to show the builder a specifically designed house or unit would have made a great deal of difference!

'And where are these two men you've invited me to meet?' she asked as they returned to the main room.

'They'll be in in a minute. Cal is just explaining the changes to the plan,' Meegan announced casually.

'Cal?'

The breath drove out of her body, so that the word came out on a forceful expiration of air. Looking dazedly around, she realised the table was set for five.

'He's such fun, I had to invite him,' Meegan was explaining as Sophie tried to regain control of her scattered senses. 'I hope you don't mind! You do like him, don't you?'

The anxious query forced her to respond.

'It's your party, Meegan, and I suppose it was a good idea to have him explain the changes to your friends.'

She took a deep, steadying breath, then continued as calmly as she could, 'The person I really want to meet is Mark. He must be someone very special for you to have become so friendly with him.'

'To have fallen in love with, you mean,' Meegan said softly, her blue gaze catching Sophie's eyes, then looking steadily at her as if to emphasise the import of the words.

'Are you really in love?' Sophie asked, a

stupid kind of betrayal shafting through her.

'I think so,' Meegan told her. 'I haven't had a lot of experience, apart from school-girl crushes on a couple of male teachers and the odd sports star when I was younger, but I'd say this is the real thing.'

Was she jealous that Meegan had found the magic of love while for her it was still a myth? Is that what she felt? Or was the sick feeling a sense of failure, a realisation that maybe there was more to life than a dedi-cation to work?

'Here are the men!'

The delighted announcement interrupted her self-analysis, and she stepped back against the wall as some unfathomable instinct urged her to run, or hide.

'Meegan told me you were pretty,' Gerald said, his eyes twinkling behind thick glasses at her as she was introduced to him. 'I like dark hair and dark eyes.'

'Me too,' said a deep voice behind her, and she swung around to face Cal Williams, who was wheeling a young man through the sliding glass doors. 'Especially when they're worn with black and silver.'

He looked devastatingly attractive, in a dark knit shirt that clung to his muscled torso like a second skin, and black tailored trousers that did nothing to hide the fact that he was incredibly fit and all man.

'A-and you must be Mark,' she stammered, stepping forward to shake hands and talking to cover the waves of uncertainty that were threatening to drown her. That great big hulk had only said that to embarrass her so she couldn't let him see that he'd succeeded. 'What do you think of the new idea for the plan? Will it be acceptable, the pole house idea?'

'It's great,' Mark assured her, wheeling himself towards the side-table where Meegan and Gerald were preparing drinks. 'Cal has gone to a lot of trouble for us. We're lucky to have such good support on the estate even before we build.'

'Did you know he has arranged for us to stay on here at reduced rates while the builders are working on the house?' Meegan asked her, reaching out to touch Mark's hand as he drew near. 'It means that Mark and I can start work right away, and be on hand to sort out any problems the builders might have.'

'And he's given us the name of his builders,' Gerald added, 'and he says I can work at the site, giving them a hand and cleaning up, things like that. The builder keeps racing pigeons.'

So 'Cal's' taken over, has he? Sophie thought sourly, then puzzled over the reference to pigeons until she remembered Meegan's remark about wanting acreage so that Gerald could keep birds. Sharing an interest in birds would be a bond between the builder and Gerald, she realised, smiling at his obvious excitement. He was a short, rather stout young man, with the clear-skinned, unlined face of a young child—and the same trusting good nature, she suspected.

'Quite the little hero, aren't I?' a deep voice whispered in her ear, sending tremors of a primeval apprehension down her spine. Was mind-reading to be added to the long list of the man's great attributes?

'As long as you don't tarnish the image by hurting them in any way,' she muttered angrily. 'Sometimes people who are willing to help out in the initial stages of a project lose interest in it after a while. Those they were helping suffer because they no longer have the support, and are also emotionally hurt because they realise that the original impulse to help was not based on disinterested friendship.'

The grey eyes that looked down at her grew cold, and she sensed a sudden stillness in the body that loomed so close to hers.

'And what might be prompting me to get involved, if it isn't simple, unbiased friendship?'

She shrugged off the chill of the words and replied crossly, 'How should I know what's in your mind? I've known people do this kind of thing to make heroes of themselves in the eyes of their friends, or to boost their own self-image. It makes them feel good, like rescuing drowning cats and helping old ladies across the road.'

'And are the acts themselves less worthy because the motive was less than pure?' He was looking down at her with a peculiar intensity in his grey eyes and she twitched uncomfortably as he added, 'And it was you who rescued the cat; I'm just the one stuck with the work of caring for it.'

'What are you two arguing about?' Meegan demanded, coming towards them with a tray of canapés. 'Whatever it is, you'll have to stop. I won't have it.'

She looked quickly around to check on

her arrangements, then added, 'Gerald is coming with drinks. This is our first combined dinner party, so you'll have to excuse the lack of co-ordination.'

She roared with laughter at her own joke, repeating it for Mark and Gerald's amusement. Sophie chuckled, although she still winced inwardly at 'disabled' jokes, even when told or enjoyed by those who lived with their own disability.

'We were arguing semantics,' Cal Williams replied casually when the laughter died down. He bent forward to take a biscuit piled with prawns and avocado from the tray on Meegan's lap. 'Dr Delano is instructing me on correct behaviour in dealing with people like yourself and Mark and Gerald.'

'There is no correct behaviour, and if you have to think how to behave then you've got it wrong. We want to be treated in the same way as non-disabled people, that's all we ask or expect,' Meegan told him. 'In fact that's what I liked about you when I met you last night. I felt that, as far as you were concerned, I was just another person wanting to build on your estate.'

Meegan smiled as if pleased with her support for him, but Cal groaned, and dropped his head into his hands.

'Now she'll think my being helpful is part of a sales pitch!'

Sophie watched his little act with a sardonic stare, and refused to say one word.

'Do you mean Sophie?' Meegan demanded. 'Why on earth would she think you had an ulterior motive in befriending us? She is one of the first non-disabled friends I ever made, and my disability has no part in our friendship.'

'Evidently she doesn't attribute the same unbiased behaviour to me,' he said sadly, shaking his head as if deeply distressed by her distrust.

Sophie felt her fingers curling with an urge to reach out and seize his broad shoulders, then, as Meegan moved away, the words blurted involuntarily from her lips. 'Sometimes I feel as if I'd like to shake you till your teeth rattle,' she growled at him, then realised the stupidity of the threat. 'As if my puny strength could move you one inch,' she added, glaring the bitterness she felt into his watchful eyes.

'There are other things beside strength that move people,' he answered obscurely, then stepped away from her to offer Gerald a hand with the drinks.

Relief flooded through her, but she kept a wary eye on his big frame as he made some remark to the two men, somehow diminishing his size so that he didn't tower over Mark, and listening intently as Gerald carefully explained his answer. He didn't seem to be putting on an act, but her suspicions remained rampant in her mind. Why should a successful, social animal like Cal Williams be taking so much trouble to nurture a friendship with these three?

'Meegan talks about you such a lot, I was glad when I found out you were living in Westport.'

Mark spoke as he glided to a halt in front of her and passed her a glass of white wine, capturing her attention with the words and looking anxiously up into her face.

'She had such a good job in the city, and such a very successful support system, that I've been worried about uprooting her and bringing her to Westport just so I can get a job.'

'She wouldn't have come if she hadn't wanted to,' Sophie assured him. 'You must know her well enough by now to know she's one stubborn lady. You might be able to lead her, if she wants to be led, but she certainly won't be pushed or manoeuvred into anything she doesn't want to do.'

'I do know that,' Mark agreed, smiling and shaking his head at the same time. 'But it still doesn't stop me feeling a bit guilty.'

'I suppose I can understand that,' Sophie replied, but she knew too little about the interpersonal give and take of love to have any panacea she could offer. She decided to change the conversation, asking Mark about his accident, and the injury it caused.

'I was lucky,' he said cheerfully, shrugging off the useless lower limbs and the wheelchair to which he was now condemned. 'I was playing football with some friends and it got a little rough. I'm still not certain what happened, but a scrum collapsed and I was caught underneath.'

Sophie felt a wave of nausea sweep over her as she realised how easily a stupid accident could deprive a person of normality— whatever that might be!

'The doctors think someone must have jumped back to get out of the mess and landed on me, and as I wasn't on the ground the weight snapped my spine. It affected the thoracic region, a T6 injury—you'd know what that means—which left me with sensory loss and muscle paralysis in my lower back and legs.'

He smiled at Sophie as if this were perfectly acceptable, although she was well aware of the problems associated with a complete spinal lesion. It was as if he was allowing her to absorb what he'd said, because he paused before he continued, 'But if I'd damaged a vertebrae in the cervical area, I'd have been a quadriplegic, and have so much less mobility than I have now, so I've reason to be thankful.'

She looked at his finely moulded features, his wavy dark hair, and intelligent amber eyes, and silently applauded his spirit. He had put the 'why me?' question behind him and was facing the future positively. Both these things had taken courage and strength.

'I think, with you by her side, Meegan can face anything,' she told him. 'And your friend Gerald seems to be an added bonus.'

She looked across to where Gerald was shifting the two unwanted chairs from the table, his face intent as he considered the best seating arrangement for his friends. To

Sophie's trained eye, he had a recognisable syndrome, although what it was and whether it was genetic she couldn't remember. Something rare, she knew that much, and obvious in the poor muscle tone, low-set ears, a slight thickening of his neck, and, she rather thought, in the tight curls that covered his head.

'He's a great guy,' Mark declared, his head turning to follow the direction of her eyes. 'If it hadn't been for him, I'd have been a very different person.'

The quiet statement intrigued Sophie, but before she could query it he was speaking again.

'He has Noonan Syndrome,' Mark explained. 'It's a fairly rare condition not necessarily associated with intellectual impairment. Although Gerald can't write and has difficulty reading, that could be because his health was bad when he was young, so he didn't get much schooling, and his eyesight is poor, which didn't help.'

'Did he grow up in a foster situation?' Sophie asked, remembering Meegan's saying something about how Mark and Gerald had met.

'No, but his mum remarried when he was

about twelve, and his stepfather's children gave him such a hard time, he asked if he could live somewhere else, which is how we ended up in the same foster home.'

Sophie was puzzled. Mark seemed so well-adjusted, it was unlikely that his family had abandoned him after the accident, so why had he been in foster care?

He must have sensed her puzzling, for he went on to explain, 'My parents have a cattle property way out west. I was at boarding-school when the accident happened, and Mum came down and stayed while I was in hospital, but she had to get back and I needed a lot of occupational and physiotherapy, so they found a couple who fostered kids with problems close to my school. By living with them during term time I could keep going there, but as a day boy, and also have my therapy. Gerald was part of their family by then, and we became good mates.'

She thought he had finished and was imagining the meeting of the two when he repeated what he'd said earlier, but in different words.

'Lucky for me I did!'

Meegan was calling them to the table, so

she couldn't ask what he meant, moving instead towards the chair that Cal Williams was drawing out for her with an over-elaborate flourish. She would look up any information she had on Noonan Syndrome at work tomorrow. She had a vague feeling that it had only recently been classified, but, try as she might, she couldn't remember a thing about it.

'Salad, Sophie?' Gerald asked, and she switched her mind away from medical puzzles and concentrated on her food. With the restricted facilities available, Meegan had managed to provide a gourmet feast— a crispy crumbed breast of chicken, which, when cut open, revealed an avocado and seafood filling, while tiny potatoes tossed in butter and a mesclun salad both comple-mented the meat.

'Cal says——' 'Cal says——' It seemed to Sophie that the two words punctuated the entire conversation. They were reference points, confirmations, laughing enunci-ations—repeated incessantly until they began to sound, in her bewildered mind, like a mantra spoken to ward off evil.

The man himself sat back and let the conversation flow, interrupting only occasionally to divert a topic or deliberately draw Sophie into the discussion.

'I'm quite happy to sit back and listen to other people talk, you know,' she told him crisply, when he had tried to involve her yet again.

'Just as you're happy to sit back and watch life go by, a spectator rather than a participant.'

Startled by this perception of her, she twisted in her seat to look at his face, trying to work out if the remark was a casually thrown dart that had happened to hit the spot or more deliberate provocation.

'My work is my life, and I'd be a failure as a doctor if I didn't get involved with my patients to a certain extent, although there has to be some restraint, some barriers,' she argued, pretending a calm indifference that was the antithesis of what she was feeling.

'Most people find that working, even at a stressful job and for long hours a day, doesn't preclude enjoying the lighter aspects of life. It doesn't automatically rule out having fun.'

'And what makes you think I don't have fun?' she demanded, incensed by his personal attack, and mortified at how near the truth he kept coming.

'You're too uptight, too tense, too much the dedicated doctor with a mission.'

He said it as calmly as she would deliver a medical diagnosis, but he had no scientific backing for his assumptions. Though she knew this and could have refuted his words, her stomach writhed with despair that he would see her that way.

'You've got to let go your inhibitions and whatever other hang-ups are tying you in knots. Relax a little, enjoy a little, live a little, Doctor, dear.'

'What are you two talking about?' Meegan demanded from across the table. 'You both look far too serious in my opinion. This is supposed to be a relaxing evening.'

Sophie smiled apologetically at her friend, while her tormentor whispered, 'I told you so!' into her ear, his warm breath causing ripples of feeling to seep across her skin.

Ignoring him, she leaned forward to speak to Gerald about the house, asking if he had ever worked on a building site before, and drawing him into conversation with a patient skill. Beside her, she could hear the murmur of Cal's voice, a deep undertone that rang insistently but indistinguishably in her ears as he talked to Meegan.

'That would be a wonderful idea,' she heard Meegan say delightedly, and wondered what the great guru had come up with now!

'The annual Lord Mayor's Ball is on in a fortnight,' Meegan said to her, as if in answer to her thought. 'Cal thought we might all go. It seems the money raised goes to various charities here in Westport, and he thought our being there might swing a little of the funding towards a pet housing project of his.'

'Might all go?' Sophie repeated weakly, looking round the table at the motley crew.

'Yes,' Cal said quickly. 'My main interest in the program to date has been housing for homeless kids, but since these three have told me about the problems people with disabilities have in finding suitable housing I believe the project could broaden its scope.'

His voice held a challenge—a goading, teasing dare to her to refuse the invitation at her own peril—but her thoughts were too disturbed to take up the gauntlet he had thrown.

Would Meegan, Mark and Gerald's attendance at the ball be necessary to swing some of the building funds into disability housing? The spectre of exhibitionism hovered over her. She knew Meegan's enthusiasm to go to the ball was prompted by her desire to do all the things her peers did, but was Cal's objective in asking them as uncomplicated?

'You will come with us, won't you, to give Meegan a hand if she needs it, and maybe even dance with me if I promise not to be wild and silly?' Gerald asked, and Sophie found herself nodding, unable to refuse when she saw the timorous beginnings of anticipation and delight in his face.

'I'll get the extra tickets and contact you later about arrangements,' Cal said quietly. 'Maybe I can repay this wonderful meal by having you over at my place for drinks before we go.'

'I've got a light wheelchair I use when I go out at night,' Meegan told him. 'The electric one is too awkward in small spaces and hopeless on a dance-floor. If I bring that do you think we could hire a stretch limo to take us and bring us home? I've never been in one before.'

Excitement sparkled in Meegan's eyes as Cal nodded.

'I'll organise it and let you know the details,' he assured her, his voice so deep and husky that it made Sophie tremble.

What was it about this man that affected her in this peculiar manner? she wondered, then remembered Meegan's remark about his constant appearances in the social pages of the paper. If the ball was only two weeks away, he would already have asked someone to go with him.

'We don't have to be in your party at the ball,' Sophie protested as the implications of the arrangement started to twist through her mind.

'Scared?' he asked, the rigid set of his face telling her it was a serious question in spite of the teasing note in his voice.

'No, I'm not, but I'm certain you've already made arrangements with your own friends and our joining your party could disrupt things.'

She watched the black brows collide above his eyes, and quaked. She had intended to be placatory, not argumentative.

'What do you mean?' he demanded in an aggressive whisper.

'W-well, four extra people, for a start,' she stammered, not knowing how to ease the sudden tension at their corner of the table.

'You don't mean that,' he growled, 'so say what you do mean. You seem to have some idea that my friends will differentiate between able and disabled people; that they will be "disrupted" simply because I invite some friends to join us who may look a little different. I think you're the one who has a problem here, Doctor, dear.'

His voice was so cold, and so hard, it seemed to chip against her flesh like an ice-pick, and the sudden realisation that he could be right made her feel very small and very vulnerable. His words had stripped away a protective coating and left nothing recognisable, nothing she could identify as herself, behind.

'I'd better be going,' she said, pushing back her chair and standing up suddenly. 'I start at five tomorrow. It was a wonderful meal, thank you, Meegan, and great to meet you, Mark and Gerald.'

She almost stumbled as she hurried to the

door, feeling four pairs of eyes on her as she made her hasty exit.

Once outside, tears streamed down her cheeks, and she shook as violently as a malaria sufferer in a fever. Her legs carried her shakily towards her car, but, having reached it, she slumped against the bonnet, unable to find the necessary energy or skill to unlock the door.

It was as if the carefully constructed whole that people knew as Dr Sophie Delano had been torn to shreds, and the pieces flung into the wind.

'Come on, I'll drive you home, then pick you up and drop you at work in the morning.'

His voice seemed to be coming from a long way off, but his arm was very real and very warm around her shoulder, and the urge to lean against him, and draw strength from his hard-packed body, was almost overwhelming.

'I didn't mean to upset you,' he said gently, leading her away from the car. 'Well, not this much, anyway.'

The arm around her shoulders squeezed her closer as he admitted, with a rueful laugh, 'But you are such a challenge! So earnest and soberly correct, and so certain in your theories and philosophies, but somehow they're all book learning, Sophie, not based on life at all.'

When he said her name, in the husky whisper he'd used earlier, she felt her bones melt, but the implications of what he was saying penetrated the fog in her brain and she fought the insidious magic he could weave about her so carelessly.

'Why?'

He had walked her unresisting body across to his car, helped her in, and reached across her to fit the seatbelt around her, as if she were a helpless child. The silence had continued until he had started the car and pulled out into the road, but now the question had come. Just the one word—why?

She knew exactly what he meant, but some remnant of her self-protective instincts remained and she muttered crossly, 'Why what?'

'Why are you like you are? Why are you so insecure that you hide behind ideas and principles that are unrelated to the real world?'

He shook his head, as if genuinely

puzzled by what he saw as her bizarre behaviour.

'That's a question based on an assumption, and if, by some highly improbable chance, your high and mightiness's assumption is wrong, then the question is unanswerable.'

She hoped she sounded more confident than she felt, automatically using words as a shield to hide her shattered self-image.

He ruined the effect of her clever speech by chuckling.

'I won't debate you, Sophie. I'm certain you have had more practice in theoretical argument, so I'd be sure to lose.'

'The great Cal Williams lose? It's unthinkable, surely!'

The words had a bite to them, but she knew they were hollow. Try as she might to keep believing her initial judgement of the man as a self-seeking, self-indulgent, pleasure-loving Don Juan, the more time she spent in his company, the more she suspected that the image was a façade as carefully constructed as her own had been. There was more to the man than she had suspected, but she had no guidelines to follow in judging him—no experience of 'life', as he'd so correctly pointed out!

'Did you live a very sheltered life because of your ethnic background?' he persisted. 'Were you not allowed to go out with the other teenagers or join in their fun and games?'

It would be so easy to blame her background that, for a moment, she was tempted. Her father had been strict with her, carefully vetting her friends and constantly reinforcing his family's moral precepts—but her mother had always been able to talk her father into anything. It was she who had convinced him that studying medicine was acceptable for a woman these days, even back in the country they had left behind.

No, she couldn't blame her family, but she wasn't about to strip away even more of her shell and reveal the truth to this man, who already saw or guessed too much. Not yet, and probably not ever!

She ignored the question, deciding that silence was the safest option, then was startled to discover that the car had stopped—right outside the block of flats that was her temporary home.

'I didn't tell you where I lived,' she said

suspiciously, swinging around to face him in the dimly lit interior of the car.

'I haf ways of knowink these things!' he drawled in an atrocious mock-film-star accent.

And suddenly all the tension eased out of her body and a smile tugged at the corners of her mouth. Maybe, if she could just relax and be herself with this man, she wouldn't get so tied up in knots!

The thought was sufficiently bizarre to make her reach for the door-handle. She wasn't even sure she knew how to relax, and she definitely wasn't convinced that she knew what 'self' she should be!

'Quarter to five do?' he asked, jolting her back to the present.

She remembered that she had no car and he had offered to drive her to work.

'It's far too early for you; I'll take a cab,' she told him, pushing the heavy door open.

'I go to work at that time anyway,' he assured her, dropping down out of his seat and walking around towards her. 'It's no bother at all.'

He held her arm as she clambered down.

'Nothing's a bother, Doctor, dear!' he said softly. 'Now, which flat?'

'I can manage without an escort!' she told him as the aura that his presence threw around her stifled her breath.

'A gentleman would walk you to the door,' he told her, keeping in step as she walked up the path towards the front entrance.

'And you're a gentleman?' she asked derisively.

'Oh, no, Doctor, dear, but from time to time I like to pretend!'

He waited until she had turned the key in the lock and stepped inside, then bowed with a low flourish, and strode off into the darkness.

CHAPTER SEVEN

STREET-LIGHTS threw islands of yellow colour on to the bitumen when she came out into the street, her heartbeat tripping erratically in spite of her forceful efforts to will it to settle. She was wearing a short, wrap-around skirt in honey-brown silk, with a long tunic top that she hoped made her look taller and slimmer. It was a dressy outfit to be wearing to work, one that she'd bought for a recent conference at which she'd given a paper on a newcomer's perceptions of general practice.

As she tried to convince herself that it was just another suit she would have worn to work sooner or later, and that its choice today was not especially significant, the big Land Cruiser swung around the corner—the man was punctual, if nothing else!

She climbed in through the door he pushed open, and settled into her seat, one quick glance taking in the tough moleskin trousers and thickly woven shirt—sensible, standard, outdoor work uniform, yet clothing that accentuated his overt masculinity.

'I'm certain you don't usually go to work at this time of the day!' she admonished him. Would the severity of her words mask the skittering, bubbling, illogical happiness she felt at the sight of his tanned face, his broad shoulders, and his long, slim fingers resting easily on the steering-wheel?

'No,' he said very seriously, then turned to grin at her. 'Sometimes I go much earlier!'

She smiled back, a treacherous warmth filling her veins, making her want to relax, to lower her defences and let fate predict the future.

You'll get hurt, common sense warned. But it's only friendship, her heart argued. It's not even that, the sensible Sophie responded. You're a kind of novelty for him, a diversion, a source of amusement for a short time! And even her heart admitted that likely truth!

'Have you been to the ballroom at the new Sheraton?' he asked, and she dragged her mind away from the internal argument.

'Not yet,' she replied, as glibly as if ballrooms were her natural habitat but she hadn't quite had time to check this one out.

'It's very grand,' he told her. 'I'm certain you'll find it matches, or possibly even eclipses, the ballroom at their city hotel.'

'Really?' she responded politely, marvelling at the composure with which she was conducting this inane conversation. 'Do they have many balls in Westport?'

'Too many, it sometimes seems, at this time of the year,' he replied, but she heard something in his voice that made her glance suspiciously across the intervening space.

Just as she thought! A muscle jumping in his cheek betrayed the fact that he was battling to hide a smile. Was he baiting her? Expecting her to protest about his frivolous social life?

'How dreary for you,' she said coolly, imitating the bored indifference of a practised socialite! 'Though, of course, it's easier for men. You can wear the same dinner-suit. What we women have to go through, with new gowns, and hair appointments, not to mention facials to help hide the dark circles under our eyes.'

'Dear Doctor!' The words erupted on a shout of laughter. 'I can just see you rushing out of the surgery, leaving a waiting-room full of patients, to have non-existent circles massaged away from under your eyes.'

They had reached the clinic and he drove into the underground car park, then turned towards her, the amusement lingering on his lips and lurking in his eyes.

'You think it's all very frivolous, don't you?' he asked, serious undertones in the words.

'Not really,' she admitted, 'but it's never been my scene. I can understand some people deriving a lot of pleasure from an extravagant social life, I just can't see myself as one of them. For one thing, I can hardly dance till dawn and then arrive at work and expect to provide an efficient service for my patients.'

'But if you arranged your shifts for a slightly later start, you could dance till midnight and still perform with your usual expertise.'

His voice was persuasive, and she was tempted to agree, but some remaining fragment of self-protection intervened and she opened the car door to escape from the subtle spell of entrancement he was weaving around her.

'I can't dance!' she said bluntly, and dropped down to the ground, hurrying to the internal staircase without a backward glance.

A report from Pathology about a patient's blood count was waiting on her desk, reminding her that, even at five o'clock in the morning, there was always book work to be done. The medical courier must have made a late call for her to have missed it last night, she decided, reading through the findings and nodding as they confirmed her suspicions of anaemia. She would have to run further tests to see if she could find a specific cause.

She rang through to the front desk and asked Emma to find Mr Wakefield's file and drop it into her box when she had the time. Muted voices told her that early morning patients were coming in, and she checked her equipment and supplies hastily, knowing the buzzer could sound at any moment.

The day brought its first problem, a young man with a throat infection, worse than it should have been because he had not sought attention earlier. She took notes as he responded to her questions about his medical history, then checked his blood-pressure and pulse, and added those to the file. She knew as soon as her fingers touched his skin

that he was feverish, and a physical examination of his neck revealed grossly swollen
lymph nodes, and the inflamed, mucus-
covered pharyngeal wall she discovered
when she examined his mouth and throat
suggested a streptococcal infection.

As she prescribed erythromycin, she
remembered a recent warning circulated to
all practitioners, and looked across the desk
at him.

'Have you been taking anything for this?
Anything that might have a drying-out
effect?'

He shook his head, the movement obviously painful.

'OK, I'll prescribe Eryc antibiotic cap-
sules, as they are the most effective against
this kind of bacterial infection, but make
sure you don't take anything other than
aspirin or paracetemol with them.'

'You serious, Doc?' he asked, obviously
intrigued by her tone.

'Very serious,' she told him. 'Taken with
certain antihistamine preparations, they can
cause a severe reaction and potentially fatal
heart problems, so don't even think of trying any quick cure that friends might
suggest.'

The thought of friends prompted another thought, and she added severely, 'And no alcohol! It undoes all the good the antibiotics do!'

He grinned sheepishly and she wondered if he'd planned spending the rest of the day down at the local hotel with his mates.

She watched him leave with another question in her eyes. He was a man not much younger than herself. How did he see her? Simply as a doctor, sitting across the table from him, or did something in him recognise that she was a woman? Did anything about her strike him as attractive? Her hair, maybe, or skin, or smile?

It doesn't matter, she told herself, but it was hard to shake off the uncertainty left in the shadow of Cal Williams' persistent attacks.

The buzzer sounded and an exasperated mother ushered in her small son.

'I've told him and told him not to ride his skateboard over the gutters,' she announced, 'but will he listen? Of course not; he always knows best. Believes nothing can happen to him, sneaks outside while we're all still in bed, and now this!'

'This' was a forearm that the white-faced

lad held gingerly in the palm of his other hand.

'I fell backwards and put my hand out behind me to save myself. It sure hurts,' he mumbled, cringing back as Sophie came towards him.

'I'll have to X-ray it to see what you've done,' she said calmly. 'You keep hold of it in the position that feels best, and come this way.'

She led the pair into the X-ray room, knowing she would have to handle the limb eventually, but unwilling to cause the boy further pain until it became absolutely necessary.

'Sit on this chair and put your arm on the table like this,' she explained to him, then gently moved the hand into position, noticing with approval the involuntary movement in his fingers as pain stabbed through him.

'It won't take long,' she assured him, pulling at the X-ray machine to position it over the arm, then inserting the photographic plate beneath it. Satisfied that all was in place, she ushered the mother outside then stepped behind the screen and pressed the control.

'One more,' she warned the youngster as she emerged.

Extracting the plate, she took it through to the developing machine and slotted it in, then returned to re-position his arm to take a lateral view of the injury.

Examining the first print, she could see the damage quite clearly—no break, but several hairline cracks that told their own story.

'Come in and have a look,' she called to the woman, leaving the transparency in its viewing frame.

'It's a greenstick fracture of the ulnar— see it there,' she said, pointing to the place where the bone had bent but not broken. 'Children's bones are less rigid, so this is more common than a clean break,' she explained. 'I'll immobilise it with a cast.'

'Will he be able to go to school with it?'

The question held so much foreboding that Sophie wondered if the mother was concerned about the lad's arm or about having him home from school for an indeterminate period of time.

'Of course he will,' she assured her. 'I'll use synthetic material, so it won't matter if he gets it wet,' she added, with an understanding smile. There was something delightfully irresponsible about the freckle-faced, red-headed imp that made her think a plaster cast would soon be in tatters. 'I'll be at least half an hour, so if you'd like to go back to the waiting-room and have a cup of coffee I'll bring him out when I've finished.'

'A cup of coffee might save both our lives,' the mother said with a grim smile.

Like the plaster cast, the thermoplastic cast was made up of fabric impregnated with a water-activated substance, but the end result was much lighter. As she wanted to immobilise both his wrist and elbow joint in order to prevent motion at the fracture site, the lightweight material would be easier for the boy to carry and less likely to cause too much wasting of the muscle beneath the cast.

She led her small and sober patient through to a treatment-room, nodding to Emma to send in a nurse as she passed through the waiting-room.

It was part of what she liked about the clinic, this ability to handle minor injuries like fractures without having to send the patients over to one of the hospitals where they invariably had a long wait before they received attention.

'This could feel hot as I wrap it around your arm; that's because of the action of the hardener drying out, and it will definitely feel wet,' Sophie explained to the boy, who had by now volunteered the information that his name was Tim, and that he was nine years old.

'I'm going to put on a shield of this soft material first; it's called stockinette, and it slips over your hand and up your arm like this.' She cut a hole for his thumb, then continued her explanations as she worked. 'Next I'll fit a bit of foam at your elbow and around your wrist so your bony bits won't rub against the cast.'

The boy nodded, his wide green eyes taking in every step of the process and, in between Sophie's administrations, examining the glass-fronted cabinets that surrounded the room, and the array of medical equipment they held.

'Now I wet this bandage, which will go hard as it dries, and wind it around like this.'

Handling the material carefully with the palms of her hands, she tried to recall all the instructions that he plaster expert at the hospital where she had trained had given her the first, second, tenth and one hundredth time she'd plastered a limb. He had been a perfectionist—an ambulance officer turned nurse who had specialised in plaster—and his explicit instructions came back to her very clearly.

With great care, she shaped the wet fabric to the injured limb, adding two plaster splints at the midline, then continuing to immobilise the wrist and thumb.

'That's the first bit done,' she told Tim, cutting off the excess cloth and neatening the edges. 'Now I'll pull the stockinette over the ends and add a few petals around that hole we left for your thumb to make sure the plaster doesn't rub against your skin.'

She turned away to find adhesive tape while the plaster was drying, cutting strips and rounding the end that she would push down under the plaster to save his skin from the hard edges.

'How does it feel?' she asked at last, smiling at the little boy, who had regained some colour beneath his freckles.

'A bit better,' he admitted, 'but it's still sore.'

'I'll suggest to your mum that she give you some Panadol to help with the pain,' she told him. 'But right now I want you to sit here for another ten minutes, just to make certain it's dry before you go. Leave it resting on the little cushion,' she added, rumpling his hair as she left the room.

'You can go in and sit with him, if you like,' she told his mother, who was still drinking her coffee in the waiting-room. 'I'd like him to sit still for another ten minutes if that's possible,' she repeated, smiling sympathetically at the harassed woman.

'He'll sit still if I have to sit on him,' Tim's mother promised, and hurried in to see her son, love and concern banishing the exasperation from her eyes.

I really know so little about human relationships, Sophie realised as she went back to her room to write up Tim's file. It is all theory, and theories can be twisted or destroyed by the human element in the equation. A sense of emptiness, of loss for something she had never had, crept over her, leaving her feeling far older than her twenty seven years.

* * *

'You taking a lunch-hour today?'

It seemed like days later that Dr Crane poked his head around the door.

'I suppose so,' she told him, stretching tiredly, 'but how we're going to find time to eat if the clinic's popularity keeps growing I don't know.'

She followed him out to the lunch area, then remembered Gerald and hurried back into her room to find a thick reference book on rare syndromes.

'New patient?' Dr Crane enquired as she dropped it on the table.

'New friend,' she explained with a smile. 'He has Noonan Syndrome, and I can't remember a thing about it.'

'Low-set ears, some degree of webbing in the neck, short stature, visual and auditory problems, woolly hair, some history of heart problems including hypertrophic cardiomy-opathy, sometimes intellectual impairment, although I know a chap in the city with it who's become a doctor.'

'You've had a patient with it,' Sophie accused.

'I have indeed! It's not common—about one in three thousand, if I remember rightly—but I'm pretty certain there are many people with it who are undiagnosed, mainly because there were no accompanying health problems and no developmental delays in the child so no reason for tests to be carried out. I belong to the Australian NS Association, if you'd like more information than that book can give.'

'I certainly would,' Sophie told him, turning to the segment she wanted and confirming what Dr Crane had told her. 'It seems it was only isolated in the early 1960s, and was at first thought only to affect males,' she read out, before adding, 'And it's a hypergonadotropic condition. Apart from some generalisations that's about all it has to say. I'm certain an association of families who have had first-hand experience will be able to offer more information.'

'Always!' the older man confirmed. 'One of the problems with knowing as much as we do is that we tend to think we know everything, and not listen to things someone else—particularly a lowly mother!—is trying to tell us. I don't believe in intuition, and I couldn't call it a hunch, but parents often become aware of something wrong with their child, without being able to explain how they know there's a problem.'

'And because they can't produce a list of symptoms we doctors tend to write them off as fussy or over-anxious!'

'Exactly! You watch that, young Sophie!' he warned. 'The secret of being a good GP is in knowing when not to talk. Listen to your patients, or to parents, especially mothers if they are the prime care-giver. And remember, you can often learn more by listening to what isn't said!'

I'm a born listener, she wanted to say, but it was too close to the disturbing conversations she'd had the previous night to be spoken of lightly in the too revealing blaze of daylight. Certain aspects of last night's events had been ruthlessly pushed to the back of her mind, to be considered when she was feeling extremely well-adjusted and secure—whenever that might be.

Calgary Williams' eruption into her life had rocked the carefully erected base of her adulthood, and she was being continually cast into the kind of physical, emotional and even intellectual disarray that her scientific mind associated with the upheavals of adolescence.

Dr Crane left the room, and returned as

she was finishing her coffee, bearing a thick file of papers.

'You might not have wanted this much information,' he said, 'but it's interesting reading, mainly because so little research has been done on NS, and most of the findings are based on parent knowledge, later tested and proved correct because of other factors.'

'Do I detect the heart of a researcher beating beneath the white coat of the GP?' she teased, and won a grin from her mentor.

'I might just get down to it soon!' he responded. 'What's retirement for, if not to do all the things one's had no time for earlier?'

'Phone call for you, Sophie. A Mr Williams!'

Kate's message brought the conversation to an abrupt end as she excused herself and hurried back to her room. What did he want now?

Apprehension made her hello sound timid, and the deep, throaty, 'Sophie?' that was his acknowledgement sent a feathering excitement down her spine. 'I wanted to talk to you about arrangements for the ball. Would you be free after work this afternoon to come over to the Sheraton with me?'

'Come over to the Sheraton?' She wondered fleetingly if she sounded as bemused as she felt. Was he organising the ball, and, even if he was, why would he want her help?

'To check it out for access,' he added patiently. 'I thought if we could find any possible problem areas that Mark and Meegan are likely to encounter we could work out ways to overcome them so that the evening isn't threatened by any awkward or unnecessary hitches.'

Why would he need me? she wondered, then, with the intuitiveness that was becoming uncanny, he said, 'I can hardly check out the ladies' washroom, now can I?'

'I'm supposed to finish at three,' she told him, unable to argue with his logic. 'I could meet you at the Sheraton any time after six.'

And give myself time to go home and tidy up, she decided, then wondered at the impulse to look her best in his company. He had given no indication that he had ever noticed her clothes, apart from that half-compliment at the motel. He certainly hadn't gone out of his way to compliment her on her best suit this morning!

'And just how do you propose to do that?' he asked, breaking into her thoughts with a mocking echo of laughter in his voice. 'No car, remember? I'll pick you up at four, which will give you an hour to finish anything that's absolutely essential.'

He didn't wait for her to argue, but said goodbye and hung up, leaving Sophie staring at the phone as she wondered how to handle this man's persistent infiltration into her life.

With the buzzer reminding her that work was waiting, she set the puzzle aside and walked out to collect the file and call her next patient. He was a middle-aged man, who limped in, then apologetically removed his sandal and proffered a rough, tanned, thick-soled foot for her inspection.

'It's one of those warts, miss,' he explained, before she could ask. 'I've tried painting it with wart stuff, but I can't get rid of it, and the damn thing hurts like hell to walk on.'

'It's a plantar wart,' Sophie told him, examining the hard lump and reddened area around it. 'They are essentially the same as ordinary rough-topped warts but the weight of the body walking round on them forces them deep into the thick skin on the sole of your foot and makes them very painful.'

'Tell me about it,' her patient quipped. 'Well, what are you going to do?'

'Cut it out!' Sophie told him positively. 'I'll give you a local anaesthetic to deaden the pain, then scoop it out with a curette, which is an instrument like a little spoon, but with sharp edges.'

'As long as I don't have to watch,' the man warned. 'I reckon you women have taken up this doctoring business because you like to see men suffering!'

He was smiling at her as he spoke, but she wondered if he was only half joking.

'We'll go through to one of the treatment-rooms,' she told him, indicating the way with a wave of her hand. 'That way I can put you on an adjustable couch and see it at eye-level.'

Kate looked up as they went through the reception area and nodded to Sophie's signal for her to send a nurse.

It was a simple operation, but the toughness of the skin made stitching the edges impossible until she had loosened the upper layers of the epidermis from the lower layers, so that she could bring the edges of the wound together without too much tension.

'Try to keep your weight off it as much as possible,' she advised the man, who nodded understandingly.

'I guess I'll bust it right open if I get about too much!'

'Well, it's not a scientific expression, but only too true,' Sophie agreed, bandaging the wound as tightly as she dared, to relieve pressure on the stitches.

As she saw her good-humoured patient leave, she marvelled again at the variety of work that general practice could provide, and felt a resurgence of her love for it, and her determination to succeed at it. So many graduates were looking towards specialisation these days, hating what they saw as petty problems, but to Sophie there was as much satisfaction in removing that painful wart as there would be in performing open-heart surgery.

'We're running way behind,' Kate warned her as she returned to her room. 'Look at the people piling up.'

The waiting-room was indeed fuller than Sophie had ever seen it. Was it the seasonal flu and the associated coughs and colds, or the growing popularity of the clinic?

Either way, she'd be very lucky to be finished by four! There was no way she could hurry a consultation. One thing at a time, she warned herself, calling in the next patient, and concentrating on the file as she showed her to a chair.

She carried the thick file on Noonan Syndrome with her when she left the clinic later, knowing there would be no time to read it during working hours. Cal Williams was propped against the balustrade at the bottom of the steps, his eyes on a hawk which was circling lazily in the air above the newly cleared land at the back of the clinic.

'Working late and taking more home with you!' he chided, tucking the bulky folder under his arm and taking her by the elbow to guide her across to his car.

Was it simply an old-fashioned courtesy, she wondered, that made him do this, or part of a macho desire to dominate? Thinking about it as he helped her into the high seat, she realised she didn't care why he did it; what did concern her was her reaction to it—the unmistakable realisation that she liked the feel of his hand under her forearm.

'What made you think of access to the

ballroom?' she asked as they drove towards the beachside hotel.

'I didn't,' he told her honestly. 'I've still a lot to learn about this disability business.'

A shamefaced grin accompanied the words, but Sophie didn't for a moment believe he was abashed. Something told her that this man had the kind of keen intelligence that would pursue knowledge for its own sake, absorbing learning as easily as a sponge absorbed water.

'I phoned my mother to let her know about the extra people joining the party, and she suggested I check it out.'

His mother's party? The thought made her feel very uncomfortable, and the feeling translated itself into aggression before she had time to stop it.

'Because she thought a number of obstacles might be enough to put you off the idea of including us?'

He shook his head—a little sadly, Sophie thought.

'You are the most suspicious, untrusting, judgemental female I have ever met,' he said slowly and deliberately. 'My mother happens to be one of those people who delight in smoothing the path of others. It was by putting herself in Meegan's place that she anticipated the possible difficulties.'

The words were dropped into a stony silence like ice-cubes clinking into a glass, and delivered towards the front windscreen as he concentrated on the traffic and the road. All she could see of his face was an angled profile and sternly tightened lips.

'I'm not very used to this!' she muttered, feeling so ashamed of herself that she could have cried.

'Not very used to what?'

'A-any of this!' she stuttered, dismayed by his withdrawal from casual friend to cool stranger and angered by her own reaction. 'I'm not a social person. I make mistakes, say the wrong things, don't know how to behave! I can't even talk to you for two minutes without saying something that makes you angry with me!'

'I'm not angry, Sophie, just puzzled!'

She waited for a further explanation but it was not forthcoming, and they drove in an uncomfortable silence towards the hotel.

Unable to bear the tightness of his lips, the sharpness of that disapproving profile, she watched his hands, noticing the bones and tendons moving beneath the skin as he manoeuvred the big vehicle into a tight parking space. As she half turned to find the door-handle, he reached out one of those long, slim hands and held her arm.

'Do all men have this effect on you or is it only me?' he asked quietly, the skin of his hand acting like a conductor, charging her with the strange electricity that only his touch could engender.

'I don't know!' she grumbled baldly, embarrassment burning its presence into her cheeks.

'Don't know?' he echoed, and she felt like hitting him. Did he want her inexperience spelt out in words of one syllable? Was he deliberately trying to humiliate her?

The thought made tears prickle against her eyelids, and she felt as weak and foolish as a small child, caught in a situation she couldn't handle.

Now he was leaning towards her, his hand lifting from her arm to her chin, his fingers sliding against her skin as he pulled her head around to face him, and looked down at her with eyes so warm and tenderly teasing that she thought her control would collapse and the tears would fall—again!

'Are you really so inexperienced?'

he asked gently. 'And if so, why?'

It was the question he had asked last night. The question she hadn't answered.

Again the treacherous thought arose, that she could blame her ethnic background, but a stubborn honesty forbade that she hide behind a lie.

'I was fat and foreign,' she said at last, a crust of belligerence in the words that dared him to laugh so that she could do battle once more.

'So fat, no one asked you out?'

The words had a disbelieving huskiness that swelled the flood of moisture burning behind her eyelids.

'But you've such an unusual face, like a Modigliani painting. Surely some of the boys you grew up with, and studied with, would have seen past your weight problem?'

Did he really think she was like a painting? she wondered, stupid delight at the compliment filling her with a rosy glow. Her mother had always told her she had good bones, but her own collisions with her mirror image had been so devastating, she had dismissed the words as parental bias.

'Didn't they?' he persisted, and she tried to remember what he had asked. 'Didn't they, Sophie?' he repeated very quietly, leaning towards her until he was so close that his lips brushed against hers, and through the blur of tears she saw a glimmer of a strange light in the grey of his eyes, a fleeting glimpse of a sun-kissed cheek, and then his mouth returned, capturing hers with a certainty that sucked all the breath from her body and made her head swim with happiness as she felt her body respond, lightening until she seemed to float above the earth, while all sensation was centred on his lips, controlling and directing her emotions as ably as a sea captain piloted his ship through a storm.

'You may not have had much experience,' he murmured against her cheek several aeons later, 'but all the right responses are there, darling Doctor, like tinder waiting for the match that will set it alight, and send it up in one glorious conflagration.'

Then his lips slid back to capture hers once again, and she fell back against the seat as the flames roared through her.

CHAPTER EIGHT

'WE'RE supposed to be looking at access problems,' Sophie said shakily.

Cal had straightened up and leaned back into his seat some minutes earlier, and it had taken Sophie that long to find enough breath to form words—words to break a silence that was intimidating her.

'Then I suppose we'd better look,' he answered easily, not turning towards her as he opened the car door and climbed lithely out. He came swiftly around the car and opened her door, then, instead of taking her elbow in the formal way he had earlier, he put his hands on either side of her waist and lifted her effortlessly to the ground. The hands lingered for a moment, their warmth pulsing through her clothing, then he drew away.

'Access, Doctor, dear,' he said, as if to remind her where they were and why they were here, although it was he who seemed to have forgotten. She followed him towards the lift, standing tensely inside it while he pressed the button for the foyer. It was swift and silent, but uncertainty was teasing Sophie's nerves to snapping point as she tried to control a body that seemed intent on pursuing its own wayward path.

'The limo Meegan has set her heart on will pull up over here,' he explained, leading the way out of the lift at a smart pace, then weaving through the scattered clumps of furniture, each grouped conversationally on the thick carpets that the designer had strewn across the sandstone-paved floor.

The front entrance was magnificent, Sophie acknowledged, seeing the twenty-foot-high glass doors that slid silently open at their approach. Tall palms in man-height terracotta pots flanked the doors, and the multiple stems of golden cane provided a lush cover in the recessed corners. There were three shallow steps leading down to the road, steps that could be negotiated with relative ease and safety, she decided. A high portico covered the area, and uniformed porters moved discreetly about, calling for cars, helping guests with luggage, opening car doors, and shutting them, all in a kind of orchestrated symmetry that reminded Sophie of a stage show.

'There's a ramp here from the road level to the footpath, and another here at the side of the steps.'

Cal drew her attention back to the reason for their visit, waving his hand towards the unobtrusive arrangement that had been provided for wheelchair access.

You must follow his lead! Act normally! she warned herself, denying the impulses to stand closer, or brush against him, or reach out and take his hand, that her body longed to follow.

'It's a modern hotel, and most architects and builders are very aware of the need for access these days,' she remarked casually, forcing herself to keep up with him as he strode back into the lobby then down a wide corridor that led off to the right.

'The ballroom is through here,' he said, opening wide double doors that led into a dim, deserted space. 'Those partitions slide back and open the two rooms into one massive one,' he explained, then his arm reached out and slid around her shoulders, and he drew her close against his side, as if he had been fighting the same impulses but could no longer withstand them.

'Oh, Sophie!' he breathed, turning to face

her and looking down at her with a twisted little smile on his face. 'You're a complication in my life I don't really need, you know.'

'*I'm* a complication in *your* life!' she said lightly, although her heart was far from easy. Inexperienced as she was, she was still aware that this was an important moment, and one false move, one hasty word, could shatter its fragility.

'Yes!' he declared, bending to brush her forehead with a kiss like the flutter of a butterfly's wing. His arms slid around her and he pulled her close against his body, so that she could feel his warmth, smell his maleness, and revel in his strength. 'Yes!' he repeated, resting his chin on the top of her head and sighing deeply.

They stood in silence, Sophie delighting in the new sensations of safety and contentment that his arms produced within her, then he moved, pushing her to arm's length and gazing soberly down at her. 'But maybe my mother can sort it out,' he added obscurely. 'Come on, we'll check the Ladies and Gents.'

The hotel would pose no problems, they decided, stopping for a cup of coffee in the plant-filled Greenery Café before they left.

Sophie took her cue from Cal, determined to appear as casually relaxed—insouciant, she decided the word was—as he. Remembering his interest, she asked about the problems of homeless youths in the town, and soon realised his commitment to the cause.

It had been wrong to write him off as a purely social animal, she realised as he drove back towards Meegan's motel to collect her car. Were her other perceptions of him as inaccurate?

'Don't look so worried!' His hand reached out to glide over her short hair, and he was smiling at her in a way that made her heart ache. 'We'll work it out!'

Work what out? And what did he think I was worrying about anyway?

Too many questions! Too much she didn't know. She cursed her inexperience and did a quick run-through in her mind of friends to whom she might be able to turn for advice. One by one they were discarded. Not close enough, too busy, different values—even Meegan would be of little help, as her inexperience, until recently, matched Sophie's own!

'I'll be in touch,' he said casually as they pulled up beside her car. 'Are you going in to see Meegan?'

Sophie shook her head.

'It's been a long day,' she said, as carefully composed as he was. 'I think I'll head straight home.'

He nodded, and, as he made no move to get out of the car, she opened the door and slid down to the ground.

'I'll wait to make sure it starts OK,' he told her as she was shutting the door, then drove forward a little way to give her room to reverse out of the parking space.

Why didn't he touch me again? she wondered as she turned the key and heard the engine fire. And why do I mind so much that he didn't? she asked herself as she fumbled into gear and backed out. I've seen enough of other people's love lives to know that men don't go around kissing women they're not interested in, yet why would he be interested in me?

They were dreary thoughts, but inescapable, and they churned in her mind, forming and re-forming in a variety of ways, generating hope, then washing it away with despair. And if he is interested in me, she wondered with a sick trepidation, why is it a problem?

The phone was ringing as she entered the flat and all the symptoms he had mentioned earlier flared in her body. Rubbing her sweaty palms on the side of her skirt, she lifted the receiver, wondering if the person at the other end could hear her heart thumping against her ribcage.

'It's Lyn from the clinic, Dr Delano,' a strange voice announced. 'Two of our doctors have phoned through sick, and I wondered if you could cover for tonight. I've got one doctor still on duty, but we like to have a second one here in case he's called out. There's a comfortable bed you can sleep in, and the receptionist will only wake you if you are needed.'

Sophie had heard of this arrangement and had often spoken with the 'sleep-over' doctor when she was finishing a late shift.

'I'll come,' she agreed, knowing they would have to have a back-up. 'What time?'

'Ten o'clock, if that's OK,' Lyn told her. 'And I'll try to get someone to do your morning session in case you have a busy night.'

'Don't worry if you can't,' Sophie said quickly. 'With all the flu about, it's not surprising we've got staff off sick. As long as I get some sleep tonight I'll manage!'

At least while she was working she didn't have to think about Cal Williams and the disruption he was causing in her life. She cooked herself a lamb chop and fixed a salad for her dinner, then had a shower, changed, and packed a small bag to take with her when she returned to the clinic.

It was only when she sat down with a cup of coffee and looked around for something to read while she drank it that she realised she'd left Dr Crane's file on Noonan Syndrome in Cal's big car.

Will he find it and drop it back to me, or should I phone him? she wondered.

She reached for the phone book, then remembered the word 'complication'. Was one of the 'ornaments' more than purely ornamental? Did he have a live-in girlfriend who would be upset if another woman phoned him?

'Bother the man!' she said to the phone book, flinging it with unnecessary force back into the drawer.

The first emergency occurred as she arrived. She was depositing her bag in the little bedroom when the buzzer by the bed sounded urgently.

'I'm Grant Stokes,' the slim, tanned doctor on duty introduced himself. 'It's anaphylaxis following a reaction to sea-food,' he explained as he pulled an endo-tracheal tube out of the store cupboard and added it to a tray he was preparing. 'She's showing signs of laryngeal oedema and respiratory distress and I want to get oxygen into her urgently, so I'm going to do an endotracheal intubation to start with.'

'It will also prevent her aspirating material from the digestive tract,' Sophie agreed, following him into the treatment-room.

She held the woman's head while Grant explained what he was doing, and slid the tube into place, listening to the chest care-fully before taping it in place and connecting it to a respirator cuff and oxygen.

'Could you monitor pulse and blood-pressure and keep an eye on the tube for slippage?' he said to Sophie.

'Joy——' he turned to the nurse who had been with the semi-comatose patient '——I want you to watch the respirator for any signs of irregularity, and use this stethoscope to listen to the chest at regular intervals. I don't want that tube obstructing one of the mainstem bronchi.'

Sophie took up her position, reacting automatically to what she knew was a real emergency. The woman's skin was covered in raised weals that she recognised as a symptom of intense peripheral vasoconstriction. A subcutaneous injection would have little chance of dispersing quickly enough to relieve the woman before her condition worsened!

Grant was drawing up epinephrine, and Sophie knew he would have to give it intravenously to relieve the bronchospasm as quickly as possible. She thought about infusion rates, knowing it was a critical factor in avoiding severe complications.

'I'm going to start a fluid drip before I give the epinephrine,' Grant told her, 'then use a one to ten thousand dilution, and administer 2mls very, very slowly. If you detect any arrhythmias let me know immediately.'

She watched, admiring the brisk, efficient movements he used to choose the fluid pack he wanted, spike it and attach it to the catheter, then insert the needle and tape the tube in place.

He is a good doctor, she decided, wondering if she would have been as quick.

'Right, here we go!' he said, wrapping a blood-pressure cuff around the patient's free arm to bring up a vein, then swabbing the blue distension, carefully inserting the fine-gauge needle, and slowly easing the drug into the patient's bloodstream.

Sophie held her breath, willing away any adverse reaction, until the tube of the syringe was empty.

'The hospital can repeat the dose in twenty minutes, if necessary,' Grant said hoarsely, as if he too had been having difficulty with his air supply.

There were a tense few minutes while they waited for the patient to respond and Sophie felt the edge of excitement that her work could often produce as knowledge challenged death.

'We're right!' Grant said at last. 'She'd have reacted by now if the epinephrine was going to increase the myocardial oxygen demand! We've done it. I'll give her Benedryl now to prevent the further release of histamines, then write a note for the hospital, telling them what we've done. They'll keep her in Intensive Care for a few hours to make sure that there's no relapse.'

He watched his patient with satisfaction, seeing already the easing of her breathing, and the slight return of colour to her lips.

'If you could remove the endotracheal tube, Doctor, and put an oxygen mask on her, the ambulance men can take over. We'll leave the drip in; they can take that with her,' he said to Sophie.

He smiled down at the stirring woman, a startling flash of white teeth brightening his tanned face.

'You'll be OK,' he said gently, patting her arm. 'But try to remember that seafood could kill you.'

Joy showed the two ambulance attendants into the room, and Sophie stood back as they transferred the patient to a wheeled stretcher and carefully angled it back out of the door.

Grant Stokes returned and handed a letter to one of the attendants, then stood and watched as his patient was wheeled away.

'Is there family we should contact?' Sophie asked, and he nodded.

'She was out with her husband and three young kids for dinner. He dropped her here and took the kids home. Poor guy is probably frantic by now. I'll go in and phone him. If he's found someone to mind the kids, he can go straight to the hospital.'

He called to Joy to bring the woman's file through to his room, and Sophie walked out into the waiting-room. Seeing the build-up of patients caused by the emergency, she walked across to Grant's door and removed the first of the files.

'Mr Cummings!' she called, opening the door to the room she used when on duty and waving the patient through. There was no way she could sleep while seven patients waited for attention. She'd help with the backlog, then go to bed.

Grant was called out to a sick child not long after the ambulance departed, and she worked her way through the list. Most were people who had been at work, and only realised how sick they were feeling once they returned home and relaxed. Some were coughing too much to be able to sleep, so had come in hoping for a quick cure.

'Is night duty always this busy?' she asked Grant when they paused between patients

for a cup of coffee about an hour after his
return.

'Not always!' he told her sympathetically.
'Quite often I get a good night's sleep!'

'Do you always do it?' she asked in
amazement, unable to understand anyone
who chose to work against their natural
circadian rhythms.

'Gives me time to surf during the day,'
he told her with the gleaming grin she'd
noticed earlier.

'That explains your tan,' she said, nodding as she looked at the smooth brown
skin. 'I've never even tried to stand up on
a surf-board. Is it really that enjoyable?'

'Is it ever!' came the swift reply. 'There's
nothing quite like it, the feeling of flying
along the top of the wave as it curls and
buckles beneath you, the sense of being able
to control, even for an infinitesimal
moment, the forces of nature through the
soles of your feet! Nothing like it in the
world!' he added, with another, more self-
conscious smile, as if his own enthusiasm
had embarrassed him.

The buzzer sounded twice in the little
lunch-room, a signal that another emergency had arrived. Coffee was forgotten as

they both hurried out to Reception to find a man, white and strained-looking, his hand clutching at his chest, and behind him a teenager with a dirty handkerchief clasped to his head, the makeshift bandage reddening as they watched.

'As you're not officially here, how about you do the ECG and I'll do the stitches?' Grant suggested, and Sophie went over and spoke to the man, and his equally anxious wife.

Collecting the file, she led them into the radiography-room, and began the routine questions and tests that might help pinpoint the source of his pain, and the possible cause.

'It's right through here and down into my arm,' the patient told her, indicating the upper region of his chest and left shoulder. 'It came on this afternoon, and I had to sit down for a while, then it went away until after I'd had dinner and was watching TV.'

'Watching TV at one in the morning?'

'Well, no. It got a bit better and we went to bed. It's just that he couldn't sleep because it was bad, and so he woke me up and I told him we'd come straight here. It's silly to be worrying yourself sick when the doctor's open down the road, I told him.'

Sophie smiled at the wifely comment, while, Query hernia? flashed through her mind, but she tucked the thought away for later. His blood-pressure was a little high, but concern over the pain could have caused the elevation. She asked about his diet, about medication, exercise and any unusual activity he might have undertaken recently.

'We did shift the bed,' his wife admitted contritely, as if she feared that her impulse to change a room around could be responsible for her husband's pain!

'Sudden strain or unusual exercise won't cause heart problems,' Sophie assured her, while her mind added silently, And nor will love, as if to remind her body that its recent behaviour had been irresponsible.

'If you take off your shirt and lie up here, Mr Smithers, I'll attach you to a machine, an electrocardiograph, which will show any abnormalities in the rhythm of the heart or changes in the strength of the beat.'

ECGs also provided the examining doctor with information about possible enlargement of the chambers and blockages in the conduction of the impulses that passed through the heart, regulating its beat, but Sophie waited until patients asked for additional information before going into further detail, as too much information could be as bad as too little for people under stress.

'I'm going to put this gel on your chest and attach leads back to the machine. The gel is a bit sticky, but it helps transmit the impulses. You lie quietly,' she warned him as she attached the first electrode at the fourth intercostal space on the right side of the sternum, then placed one opposite it. The fourth electrode went above the fifth intercostal space, with the third midway between it and the second.

Once she had these positioned, it was easy to place the last two on the same level as the fourth, one on the anterior axillary line and the last on the mid axillary line, making a rough arc on the left-hand side of his chest. The six leads would provide the preliminary information, but any irregularity would mean taking a second reading using twelve leads.

As the patient lay quietly, Sophie watched the strip of paper issuing from the machine, allowing it to form a small patterned ribbon before she lifted the end and began to study it.

The vertical and horizontal gridlines made up tiny boxes, with twenty-five horizontal boxes for each second recorded. The vertical boxes recorded voltage, so the normal pattern was familiar to the nurse or doctor operating the machine, although extra skill was required to diagnose problems from an atypical reading.

'It looks fine, Mr Smithers,' Sophie told him. 'Everything ticking along in the best possible pattern, although if you like I can arrange for you to have a stress test.' She detached the electrodes, and wiped the gel from his chest. 'That involves another ECG being taken while you exercise on a treadmill. It would pick up any latent problems not shown on the resting ECG.'

'Perhaps he'd better do that,' his wife responded. 'After all, the pain is real enough. He went as white as a sheet when it started.'

'It could also be a hiatus hernia, a problem that often provides the same deep, steady pain symptoms as heart problems,' Sophie suggested. 'Do you suffer much heartburn, indigestion or gastric reflux?'

'He's always swallowing Quickeze.' Mrs Smithers answered again, while her husband nodded his agreement, obviously happy for her to be acting as spokesperson.

'Then a hiatus hernia is a possibility. What happens is that the junction of the oesophagus and stomach, which usually sits neatly in below your diaphragm——' she used a scrap of paper to illustrate her words '—moves up here like this. The little loop can cause some of the stomach contents to be forced back up the oesophagus and that irritates the lining and produces the symptoms, particularly that burning, tight sensation that you have probably been feeling.'

'It did come on after meals both times,' her patient agreed. 'So what do I do about it?'

'Do you want to go back to your own doctor and talk to him about this? If you do, I'll send him a copy of the ECG.'

Sophie made the suggestion knowing that most after-hours patients had a regular GP and were only using the clinic because it was open all night. That had been the purpose of it, after all!

'I'd just as soon come back here, if you

can do that stress test thing here?'

'We can,' she assured him. 'And when you come back we can talk about further tests for hernia. In the meantime, try eating smaller meals and eating more often, and avoid fizzy drinks, highly seasoned food, caffeine and alcohol.'

'Doesn't leave much!' he grumbled, but his smile told Sophie that he would at least think about her advice.

'Can I make another appointment for him as we go out, or should I phone the clinic tomorrow?' Mrs Smithers asked.

'You can make it tonight. The receptionist will fix it for you. Any of the doctors here would be happy to do the test.'

She hid the yawn that was threatening and fixed a cheerful smile to her lips. Surely things would be quiet enough for her to go to bed for a while now?

'He'd rather come back and see you,' Mrs Smithers told her, and Sophie looked at Mr Smithers, who nodded his agreement and smiled shyly.

She walked back to Reception with them, then correctly interpreted Lyn's shooing movement as a signal to go to bed. Only one patient sat in the waiting-room, and

Grant would be able to deal with him. If she waited until it was totally empty, she could be up all night!

Grant had a standing order for fresh rolls and bagels from a local bakery, and she tucked into these with him before he went off duty, enjoying his undemanding company.

'Do you see much of the other staff when you work day shifts?' he asked, and Sophie shook her head, her mouth full of crispy roll and honey.

'Apart from Dr Crane, who tries to take the same lunchtime, it's a hello and goodbye in the foyer, or an urgent consultation with a patient waiting, when something unusual crops up!'

'Do you find it lonely?'

Sophie looked enquiringly at him, wondering what he saw in her to make him ask the question.

'No,' she said slowly, testing the word for honesty as she spoke. 'I enjoy the patients coming and going, the contact with the reception and nursing staff. To me, it's exactly what I've always imagined it would be, apart from the days when the line of patients never seems to end.'

'Days and nights!' he agreed, with his charming grin. 'Well, the surf is calling! I hope we run into each other again sometime,' he continued. 'You know where the shower is, of course!'

She nodded again, and waved goodbye. She would need a long, cool shower to help her wake up before she tackled the morning's work. Four and a half hours' sleep was not enough, even if she hadn't been dancing the night away!

'There's a message for you to ring a Mr Williams as soon as you have a free moment,' Emma told her some hours later, poking her head around Sophie's door as she saw a patient walk out. 'He's called three times, so I guess it could be urgent.'

The rules for personal calls were simple, and only the lucky caller who found the doctor they wanted on a coffee- or lunch-break was ever put straight through. Otherwise, the reception staff took messages, and the doctor phoned back between patients.

'I'm stopping for lunch after the next patient, so I'll phone him then,' Sophie told her, pretending to herself that the shaky feeling his name evoked was only hunger.

'Where were you last night?' he demanded the instant he heard her voice. 'I called at your flat to drop off the file you left in the car, and you were out. I rang every half-hour until midnight,' he added, reproach and suspicion mixed in even parts in his voice, 'and even rang Meegan to see if you'd gone back over there!'

Later on she would be sure to think of something clever to say in reply to his insistent questioning, but she was so bemused by the attack that she simply sat, not wanting to say she was at work because he had already berated her for working too much overtime, and would certainly have plenty to say if he realised how long she'd been on duty.

Dr Crane came in and she motioned to him that she would only be a minute. He walked towards the window and stood there, looking out at the scarred hillside.

'Well?' Cal asked, and she knew she would have to answer. He was like a dog with his teeth sunk firmly into a bone, and not likely to give up for any reason.

'I had to go out,' she said briefly. 'I'm sorry I missed you, but if you could drop the file into the clinic I would be very grateful.'

There was a silence, and she wondered what he was thinking, how he was reacting. Would his next words tell her anything?

'I thought we might have dinner this evening.' There was a pause, then he went on abruptly, 'Talk about the arrangements for the ball. I could return the file then.'

Tonight? When it was just lunchtime and she had another four hours' work to get through! All she wanted to do tonight was go home and go straight to bed.

'I'm sorry,' she said softly, regret and relief vying with each other for supremacy in her emotions, 'I can't make it tonight.'

'I understand,' he returned with a short bark of a laugh. 'I'll be in touch.'

She hung up with a sigh, and found the older doctor's eyes on her, a sympathetic smile turning up the corners of his lips.

'The boyfriend?' he asked.

'Hardly that!' Sophie told him. 'He's just a fellow I met the other day through a friend.'

'And now he's asking you out.' Dr Crane continued to study her undoubtedly flushed face. 'Not making a nuisance of himself, I hope?'

'Oh, no!' Sophie assured him. 'I just don't understand why he keeps wanting to see me, unless. . .'

'Unless?'

'Well, there are only two possible reasons.' She spoke quickly, as if glad of the opportunity to verbalise her feelings. 'The first is that I'm providing a little light amusement in his life; I'm sufficiently different to have novelty value and he's toying with me the way a cat toys with a mouse. And the other is that he's a genuinely kind person——' something inside her wanted to laugh uproariously at this conjecture—and he's trying to make me feel at home in Westport!'

Dr Crane continued to study her face, but said nothing, and his silence prompted her to speak again.

'And why he'd be upset when I said no is beyond me!'

'Is it, Sophie?' her visitor asked, a chuckle buried in the words. 'He'd be upset if he asked for a more normal reason than either of those your suspicious mind has dredged up,' he told her. 'Have you considered the third alternative—that he's asked you out because he likes you? That he's a man and you're a woman and he finds you attractive?'

'Me, attractive?' Sophie echoed. 'Not in this man's eyes! He's more into the slim, svelte model type, from all I hear.'

'Don't underrate yourself, Sophie,' the other doctor said firmly. 'Apart from the fact that you have lovely brown eyes, two cute dimples, a good brain and a pleasant personality, you must remember that there's a little bit of something special, a subtle magic, in every person. It just needs the right eyes to see it—the eyes of love!'

'Cal Williams' eyes aren't the eyes of love!' she said emphatically, quelling the stupid flicker of hope that Dr Crane's words had set alight.

'Cal Williams? This man you've just refused to have dinner with is The Cowboy?' His astonishment would have been funny if it hadn't pierced through the little bubble of happiness that his compliments had left within her.

'Why, he's the most sought-after bachelor in town, you know—the man that all the girls would like to rope and break in, so to speak! Even my daughter——'

The doctor stopped abruptly, obviously

realising that his remarks were verging on gossip, and insensitive as well.

'There's no reason why he wouldn't find you attractive,' he added stoutly, but Sophie sensed the lie.

In this man's opinion, Cal Williams was way beyond her league!

CHAPTER NINE

NOT seeing him was worse than seeing him,
Sophie decided three days later, when her
body ached from the tension of waiting for
a message, and was stiff with the strain of
willing her phone to ring.

It's a stupid infatuation, she told herself,
when her intelligence failed to control the
unease within her and she felt she had to
rationalise it.

The file on Noonan Syndrome that she
had left in his car had been dropped back
at the reception desk, but no message had
accompanied it, except the unspoken rebuff
of there not being a message.

I should have told him I was at work, she
would think, then argue with herself over
the choices she'd had, although it was
already too late for it to matter. For the first
time in her life the dreaded words 'if only'
loomed up and haunted her as she dreamed
impossible dreams and tried to relive the
past in her imagination.

'Cal's hurried through the council

approval and arranged with the builder to start next week.' Meegan's voice bubbled with excitement as she poured out the news.

Sophie listened, making appropriate responses on her end of the phone, while she discovered another phenomenon. Even hearing his name made her heart skip a beat, she realised, then felt a tinge of totally irrational betrayal that Meegan had seen or been speaking to him, while she hadn't.

'It is ridiculous! Ridiculous! Ridiculous!' she said aloud, once she'd put the phone down, then decided to drive over and visit Meegan at the motel, denying that the thought had been prompted by the fact that he might also be there.

'Ridiculous!' she kept repeating to herself as she drove. 'Ridiculous!' she said again, when disappointment churned within her as she scanned the car park at the motel and did not see his big vehicle.

I can't believe I'm doing this, the rational part of her mind said, but she parked her car while hope renewed the tension in her heart.

'Meegan and Mark are out!'

Gerald's voice came from the door of the

next unit as she knocked a second time on Meegan's door.

'It's Sophie, Gerald,' she called back, walking away from the door and hesitating on the path. 'I was driving by and thought I'd call in and say hello.' Her fingers were crossed behind her back as she made the feeble excuse!

'You can come and say hello to me, if you like,' he said quickly, and Sophie sensed a loneliness that mirrored her own.

'I'd be happy to,' she told him, stepping across the low ground cover between the two paths and following him through the open door.

'Mark and Meegan need some time together without me,' he told her, as if repeating a lesson he'd just learned, and she wondered if he had been telling himself the same thing before she arrived.

And that's like me telling myself I don't care about Cal Williams not contacting me.

'Would you like a cup of coffee?' Gerald asked, and, anticipating Sophie's nod, he picked up the kettle and hurried into the bathroom for water to fill it. His movements were precise, as if the simple skills involved had been carefully taught and perfected with practice.

'Mr Phillips, the builder, keeps racing pigeons,' he told her as he put coffee and biscuits on the small table by her armchair. 'I met him on Tuesday and next week, after work one day, he's going to take me to his house and show me.'

Sophie smiled at his enthusiasm.

'I know nothing about racing pigeons,' she admitted.

'I don't either,' Gerald confessed, 'but Cal says there's no reason why I can't keep them too!'

Oh, does he now? Sophie thought, pleased to have found a grievance against the man to divert her attention from memories of his fine, clear skin, gleaming grey eyes and thick, dark hair. And what made him think Gerald would be able to cope with racing pigeons?

'You home, Gerald?'

His voice sent her heart cavorting around inside her chest, and she shakily returned her coffee-cup to the table before she spilled the entire contents down the front of her second best suit.

It's what you hoped might happen, sensible Sophie reminded her drily, annoyed with all the jumbled manifestations of surprise and idiocy and anger spinning from the uncontrolled part of her mind and body.

'Hello, Sophie,' Cal said calmly as he walked into the room and clipped Gerald on the shoulder with a friendly punch.

'I'll get you a coffee, Cal,' Gerald said quickly, and disappeared back into the bathroom with the kettle.

'You might be encouraging Gerald to get into something more than he can manage with racing pigeons,' she said, then realised she sounded more abrasive than she'd intended as she fought an urge to smile and simper and gaze at him like a moonstruck cow!

'Can I do nothing to please you?'

The words grated across her skin and she flinched back in the chair. She was shamed by her unprovoked attack on him, yet she knew it was the only way she could pretend she didn't care.

'I was telling Sophie about the pigeons,' Gerald announced as he returned and began the ritual of making another cup of coffee. 'Cal is going to help me train them to come home,' he continued, compounding Sophie's embarrassment. 'After they get used to their perches, you have to let them out for a short time each day, then after that you take them about a mile from home for a——What do we call letting them go like that, Cal?'

'A toss, Gerald. They have to get used to the travelling baskets first, then they are tossed once a week for a few weeks, increasing the distance until it's time for their first long flight.'

He ignored Sophie but she sensed he was showing off his knowledge to punish her for her doubts.

'I wouldn't have thought training pigeons was part of a cowboy's accomplishments,' she responded lightly as she fought desperately for the control to carry on a rational conversation with these two.

'Cowboys can do anything!' he assured her, his lips set in such a grim line that she knew he hadn't forgiven her earlier comment. 'I've spoken to Tim Phillips and he has a breeding pair you might like to start with, Gerald. He also knows of another breeder who will have young 'uns soon.'

'That's great, Cal,' Gerald responded, and Sophie saw the bright excitement in his eyes and prayed he would not be disappointed if he undertook this project and failed.

'It's like the old saying "'Tis better to have loved and lost. . ."' Cal whispered to Sophie as if reading the doubt that lingered in her eyes.

'Than never to have'—not 'loved', in this case, but tried! she thought. Is it, though? she wondered, her mind jolting between pigeons and love as she continued her internal battle against the new longings and desires that raged within her.

'Cal says I should see everything, even go out with the truck driver one day to let the birds go,' Gerald told her, and Sophie, wincing at the 'Cal says', nodded and prepared to be told all that Gerald had learned about pigeon racing.

'I think Sophie's getting tired,' Cal said an hour later, interrupting Gerald's explanations gently but firmly. 'I'll walk her to her car. Thanks for the coffee, Gerald.'

And with that she was moving towards the door, his hand grasping her elbow, warm and curiously intimate.

'Goodnight, Gerald,' she said as calmly as her breathless state would allow.

'Which of us is shaking, Sophie?' he

asked, his voice so deep and husky that it made the hairs on her arms prickle to attention. They were walking along the shadowed path towards the parked cars, but their steps slowed, and then stopped, and his arms enfolded her, drawing her close into his body, while a sigh as soft as angel wings fluttered in the air above her head.

It was the last intimation of softness! The kiss that followed, the lips that sought and captured hers, held a burning hunger that seared across her soul and held her ransom to his touch.

She heard the groaning of anguish and frustration, and recognised the cause—but did not know who made the noise, or if it had been a chorus.

His hands, hot and demanding, flowed across her back, moulding her against his body, pressing her pliant form into his hardness like a sculptor shaping his clay. She felt her flesh melt against him, and revelled in her softness flowing out to meet his bone and muscle, and all the while their lips clung, drawing sustenance from each other with a desperation that bordered on madness.

'I was at work,' she muttered into his

chest, after the kiss had finished and they stood, entwined, dragging air into depleted lungs. 'The other night—I was called into work.'

She didn't know why she was saying this—didn't know anything any more! The words had just come out!

'I know that now,' he said, his arms tightening around her so that she could scarcely breathe. 'But it's still no good, Sophie! It's madness! Crazy! Insane!'

She had no idea what he was talking about, yet could understand. What she was feeling could only be described as insanity. Or was love like that?

She shook her head against his chest—slowly—sadly! If only she knew!

'My mother will be in touch with you about the ball,' he said into her hair after a long yet strangely comfortable silence. 'She means well but don't let her bully you.'

Now she nodded, not knowing what to say, and reluctant to break the spell he had woven around her as surely as he held her in his arms.

Lights splashed across the car park, seeking out their dark patch of shadow beneath the trees. He turned her in his arms and led her to her car, taking the keys from her nerveless fingers and bending to unlock the door.

'Are you OK?' he asked as she sank into the driver's seat. His fingers slid softly along her skin, down her arm and across her fingers, as if reluctant to lose physical contact, and the trail they left burned with the memory of their touch.

'I'm fine,' she lied, knowing that she would never be the same again, recognising the force of love and acknowledging its existence with reluctance and apprehension.

It was a curious sensation, she decided, analysing it many sleepless hours later, perhaps because, for the first time in her life, she was being swept along a path not of her own choosing, and, fight it as she might, there was little she could do. It was the fearful inevitability of it that frightened her, yet fear could not halt the excited skipping in her heart as she murmured his name, nor still the tremors of desire that flared through her body when she remembered his touch.

'Could you do a sleep-over next week?' Dr Crane was working out rosters when she walked into the clinic to start the day's work. 'I don't like to have to ask you, but one of the other doctors is taking holidays and another who's been filling in here has finally been accepted on to a specialty program.'

'As long as it's not Friday night,' Sophie told him, her face splitting into an involuntary grin as she experienced the delight of anticipating something special.

'Going to the Lord Mayor's Ball?'

'I am!' she said, still smiling foolishly. 'I've a friend shifting down here from the city, and with two of her friends we'll be quite a party.'

'And I suppose you'd like Saturday off as well?' Dr Crane teased good-naturedly.

'I worked last Saturday,' Sophie reminded him. 'One a month is supposed to be the rule.'

'But you've always been happy to do extra weekend work,' Dr Crane reminded her.

'I still don't mind,' she assured him, although as she walked through to her consulting-room she wondered. She would have liked to feel more certain about that statement, more committed, as she had been in the past. Whatever had happened, or was

yet to happen, between herself and Cal
Williams, would she ever be the same
again? Would work be enough, or would
some part of her spirit, freed by this
strange, late-blooming, adolescent fancy,
want more from her life than a dedication
to work?

'You've seven return appointments
today,' Kate told her proudly, bringing in a
list of familiar names and a pile of files.
'We'll still give you patients without
appointments in between, and leave you to
call these through when they arrive.'

Sophie took the files and thanked her,
knowing that she would have time to read
through them before she started work, and
check that test results were available where
necessary. A feeling of satisfaction stole
over her, as if these seven patients had all,
in some way, given her praise.

David Ambrose—this would be his last
visit as his hand was now healing well, but
she would see him again, she knew, for his
wife had brought their daughter in for her
five-year-old triple antigen, and promised to
return whenever any of them needed a
doctor.

Mr Wakefield—she recalled the tired,

lined face of the elderly man who had been one of her first patients at the clinic. She had sent him for an endoscopy at the local day hospital to check for any upper gastro-intestinal tract bleeding that would explain his anaemia. The results showed that the endoscope had revealed some polyps with a query pre-malignancy. The surgeon had cauterised the polyps and would check again in six months. She would reassure Mr Wakefield, and also arrange for another blood test, to see if his red cell count had improved, or if further tests should be done—if he wanted them.

Offer the patients choices, she reminded herself. Don't bulldoze them into doing what you think might be best for them.

The thought brought Cal's face vividly to mind, and she shuddered as she realised how easily he could enter her thoughts and interrupt her day. The buzzer sounded on the door and another day began.

A middle-aged woman responded to her call for Miss Cameron, and came towards her holding her right hand carefully in her left.

'Problems with it?' Sophie asked sym-pathetically.

'It's almost stopped working!' her patient replied with obvious disgust. 'Here I am at fifty-five and never been to a doctor in my life, and now my hand's stopped working.'

Sophie dropped the bare file on her desk and turned to take the offending, work-roughened extremity in her hands, feeling the tension and noting a slight wasting of the small muscles around the thumb.

'Does it hurt all the time?' she asked as she turned it over and felt for swelling that would cause compression of nerves in the compartments of the wrist.

'Yes, but I can put up with that,' the woman told her. 'The problem began ages ago, with a bit of pain, and a sort of tingling in my thumb and these fingers.'

She indicated the three adjoining fingers, and Sophie reached for a pin to test loss of sensation in the digits.

'What's happened now is I can't seem to grasp anything with it. Can't do this!' She tried to reach out and close her fist, but gasped with the intensified pain. 'And how can I milk my goats if I can't close my hand?' she demanded, obviously more distressed than her gruff exterior betrayed.

'You keep goats?'

Sophie's amazement seemed to annoy her patient, who replied very caustically, 'This wasn't always a seaside mecca for the wealthy. Before Cal Williams started cutting up his father's old farm and all the other farmers in the area saw a way to make easy money, this was a rural community.'

'Do you sell the milk?' Sophie asked, still amazed by the idea of a goat farm within easy reach of the clinic.

'Sure do! I've a special licence to produce it. Health food shops take all I can supply. With all those allergies around that people get, goat's milk is in demand.'

There was a brusque satisfaction in the words, and Sophie smiled at her.

'If that's what has kept you so healthy, I should be recommending it to all my patients. Now, tell me what you feel when I do this.'

She tapped her finger in the centre of her patient's wrist and waited expectantly.

'It makes my fingers tingle,' Miss Cameron announced. 'But they do that most of the time anyway.'

'I think it's what we call carpal tunnel syndrome,' Sophie explained. 'There's a little passage through your wrist where the median and ulnar nerves, and most of the tendons from the arm, pass through to the hand. A strong strap called the transverse carpal ligament lies across here——' she drew a line across the front of the wrist '—to stop them bowing forward when the wrist or fingers are bent.'

She looked at her patient and received an encouraging nod.

'There's not much space between this ligament and the median nerve that goes to your thumb and fingers, and if any swelling occurs it presses the nerve against the ligament and you get pain and loss of sensation, especially in the thumb and adjoining fingers.'

'Carpal tunnel syndrome!' the woman announced, then shook her head. 'Why should it swell? Have I injured it? And why this hand, which is the one I need the most?'

'Water retention can cause swelling, and unfortunately, as with everything mechanical, the bits that are used most often are usually the bits that break down.'

'But I need to be able to use it,' Miss Cameron protested. 'What's the answer?'

'Surgery would relieve the pressure and

the muscles activated by the nerve usually recover their function, but there are other alternatives you could try first if you like.'

'Hit me with them!'

Sophie grinned at the valour in the words. Someone who had never been to a doctor in her life could well be very wary of surgery!

'I could prescribe a diuretic for you; that would reduce water retention and help relieve the pressure. Sometimes it helps if you keep your wrist in a rigid splint, especially at night, and I could also try an injection of local anaesthetic and corticosteroid, into the area but away from the nerves.'

'They all sound like maybes!' Miss Cameron said, and Sophie nodded.

'So much of medicine is,' she agreed. 'What works for one person will only aggravate the problem in another, so we can't ever say, This will happen, with any certainty. But about forty per cent of cases can be relieved without surgery.'

'And with surgery?'

'As long as there hasn't been long-term compression, the results are usually excellent, and the likelihood of it recurring is very small.'

'I'll go away and think about it,' her patient announced. 'And I'll try the splint and some of those tablets you mentioned while I'm thinking, just in case that cures it quickly.'

Again Sophie smiled at the redoubtable woman.

'Don't leave it too long,' she warned as she wrote out a prescription. 'The longer the nerve is compressed, the more chance there is of permanent damage to the small muscles that move your hand and fingers.'

'I'll come back later this week,' Miss Cameron promised, waving the prescription at Sophie as she hurried to the door.

The waiting-room was filling up, she noticed as she called the next patient in, and work continued, keeping her too busy to think of any of the new distractions that were shadowing her life. It was two o'clock before she stopped, hurrying through to the lunch-room for a late break before facing her afternoon patients.

'Meegan phoned you earlier,' Kate told her, coming into the room and dropping into the chair beside her. 'She wanted to know if you could finish early one day this week to go shopping with her. I told her you were off at four today and I'd send you straight home.'

'Kate!'

'Well, you need a push to get you moving. The other staff here don't work all the extra hours that you put in, and when there's someone like you around other people take advantage.'

'Other people?' Sophie queried, smiling at this unexpected championship.

'Some of the doctors here never work weekends, and quite a few are late every day!'

Kate sounded as shocked by this dereliction of duty as Sophie was herself, but she excused them with a quiet, 'Oh, some of them have young families, and other ties that I don't have.'

'Well, I don't know about that,' Kate grumbled. 'Anyway, I'll see you don't have any late patients today so you can go shopping with your friend.'

'Thank you, Kate,' Sophie said quietly, and smiled as she watched the other woman march out of the door, while a skittish excitement as foreign to her as leprosy coursed through her blood. She was going shopping with Meegan after work—going shopping for a ballgown! It was like all the fairy-stories rolled into one, and images of ugly ducklings vied with Cinderellas to make her head spin with intoxicating delight.

'Why this shop, Meegan?' she asked as her friend directed the accessible taxi to stop outside an elaborately plain shop front with one elegant gown draped in the window. A discreetly lit interior gave an impression of expensive exclusivity.

'You'll see,' Meegan told her as the taxi driver undid the straps that held her chair in place and lowered the ramp so that she could roll out on to the footpath. 'It's accessible, for one thing!' she added, pointing to the gentle slope leading up to the front door.

'I'll give you ladies till closing time,' their driver called after them as the doors of the shop slid open electronically.

'You must be Meegan!'

The tall, dark-haired woman walked swiftly forward, bending to grasp Meegan's hand and shake it warmly.

'And you are Sophie?' The question had

a mixture of surprise and incredulity underlining each word. Then she said obscurely, 'I see!' and walked around the pair of them looking extremely doubtful.

'I know exactly what would suit you, Meegan. Come through here to the dressing-room. Will you leave your chair outside? Shall I get Janey to help you dress or would you prefer to do it yourself?'

Meegan was marshalled across to a curtained alcove as big as the kitchen in Sophie's flat, and a young woman, obviously Janey, summoned to stand by. Something about the proprietor's organising skills rang a bell in Sophie's mind, but she was too bemused by the little scene being acted out in front of her to pursue the fleeting impression.

The tall woman was now moving purposefully along the racks of clothes, pushing aside this one, tugging at that, and pulling out her carefully approved selections.

'Take these, Janey,' she ordered, and again a sense of familiarity twisted through Sophie's mind. 'Put them in the changing-room for Meegan and stay there in case she needs a hand with zips or buttons.'

She waved to Meegan to get moving, adding, 'You can try them all but I bet the silver will be perfect!'

Her satisfied nod seemed to finalise that issue and she turned back to Sophie, energy brimming from every movement although she must be close to sixty.

'You're looking confused, poor child,' she said kindly, and reached out to take Sophie's hand and pat it. 'Didn't Meegan tell you? I'm Janet Williams!'

No wonder her manner had seemed familiar, Sophie thought through a wave of nausea. How could Meegan do this to her?

'Sit down, my dear,' Mrs Williams was saying, drawing her towards a low, brocade-covered *chaise-longue*. 'Cal tells me you work far too hard. You rest for a moment. Would you like a cup of tea? Coffee?'

Sophie shook her head dazedly.

'I'm fine,' she said, although she was still feeling faint and totally bemused. 'I'll just sit here and wait till Meegan's finished.'

'Oh, but you'll need a gown as well,' Mrs Williams protested. 'It's a very special night in Westport, and as it will be your social début in town, if you know what I mean. . .'

Début and finale, Sophie thought, but she

knew the woman was being kind. Besides, she would need something to wear! That was why she was out with Meegan—but now? Somehow the excitement had vanished in the shock of meeting this assured, elegant, managing woman who was Cal's mother.

'I'd thought, when Cal described you, that it would definitely have to be black or white, but now I see you I'm not so certain. A deep cream perhaps, or maybe. . .I think I know!'

She darted off, flitting along the racks of peacock colours again.

Sophie heard the words and knew they were directed at her, but her concentration had been lost at the beginning of the sentence with the phrase 'when Cal described you'. He'd said something one night about his mother being able to sort it out. Was he talking about some physical transformation? Would he be ashamed to be seen with her in public looking like the frump she undoubtedly was?

Pain and shame swept over her—and disappointment, and a sense of betrayal!

'You might like to look at them all yourself, and you don't have to buy anything here, but I would really like to see you in this.'

The woman was back, a tentativeness in her voice that Sophie sensed was very rare.

'This' was a slim-fitting slip of a dress in a soft, deep blue material that shone with a dull lustre in the clear light. Swirling about it, from waist to hemline, was a filmy rainbow mix of colour, emerald and purple, gold and silver, all twisting through the gauzy material to give it a beauty and life that was breathtaking.

'I'm too plump to wear a figure-hugging sheath like that,' Sophie said, although her hands had moved out to touch the soft overskirt, and finger the rich material of the dress.

'It's your size,' Mrs Williams said firmly, 'and if you've been telling yourself you're too plump for years, then you've probably never tried on a sheath. I think you'll find that they are very flattering for someone who has a decent shape. It's the rake-thin, beanpole, model types that look bad in something straight, although no one likes to say that these days.'

Wincing at the description 'decent shape', Sophie stared at the dress, tempted beyond will-power, yet reluctant to try it.

It was so beautiful! What if she tried it on and made it look terrible?

'It will look fantastic on you,' Mrs Williams said, with the same uncanny perception that her son had often shown. 'You are a beautiful woman, Sophie, although you may not know it yet, as it's a beauty that comes with maturity and will last forever.'

She spoke so sincerely that Sophie looked up into her face, searching for a sign of glib salesmanship in the words. The grey eyes were so like his that she shivered, yet she could see the sincerity, and kindness, in the woman's face, and knew she could trust her words.

'What do you think?'

Meegan broke the moment by rolling forward, a vision of silver tulle and frothy ribbons, eyes sparkling and cheeks pink.

'I think you look like the fairy on the top of the Christmas tree—absolutely beautiful!' Sophie cried, rising to her feet and hurrying over to examine the beautiful creation and the startling transformation in her friend.

'It is lovely, isn't it?' Meegan said shyly, and Sophie saw tears in her eyes. Meegan had put aside her bitterness, but there must be times when she wished for strong, straight limbs, and muscles that worked at her command.

'Mark will be knocked right off his feet!' Sophie assured her, and was relieved when her weak joke was greeted by a shout of laughter, and the misty regret vanished from Meegan's eyes.

'Oh, Sophie, are you going to try that on?' she asked in awestruck tones, seeing the gown that Mrs Williams still held. 'It is so beautiful!'

'Too beautiful for me, I think,' Sophie told her, but Meegan's protests and Mrs Williams' firm insistence drove her towards the dressing-room, the gown held at arm's length, as if she was afraid she might contaminate its beauty.

The sheath slipped over her head, and fitted snugly along her body, caressing it with the softness of silk satin. The dark blue emphasised the creaminess of her skin, but the effect was a bit voluptuous, she decided, tugging at the bodice to try to cover the deep cleft of her breasts and the visible mounds of softness rising out of the neckline.

Twisting and turning in front of the mirror, she tried to decide if her bottom stuck out too much, or if her hips looked too large, but it seemed that Mrs Williams might have been right. The dress had definite slimming ability, and the Sophie in the mirror looked taller and more elegant than the real Sophie had ever seen her.

Sophisticated, too, she decided, pushing her hair back with her hands to give it an upswept look, and feeling a tiny trickle of excitement returning. She could wear this dress anywhere, she decided, and it was a classical style that would never date.

She nodded at her image, then reached out and picked up the filmy overskirt, fastening it about her waist then twirling in front of the mirror to see the effect. It transformed the classical, restrained gown into a frivolous concoction—a mad, beautiful, have-fun-in garment that switched the image in the mirror from svelte sophisticate to party girl.

'It's definitely not me!' she said aloud, then watched as Mrs Williams slipped through the curtain and stood reflected behind her.

'Every now and then we all have to throw off our image of ourselves, and let all the other people inside us have a chance at a little fun,' Mrs Williams told her, nodding her approval at the transformation.

'But. . .'

'No buts, Sophie, it's beautiful, and so are you. I couldn't sell it to anyone else because no one would look as good in it, so you'll have to buy it for my sake, won't you?'

The words were accompanied by a charming, teasing, conspiratorial smile that reminded Sophie so much of Cal that she sighed and nodded, swept along on the tide of effervescent energy that these Williamses generated.

CHAPTER TEN

SOPHIE dressed for the ball with shaking fingers, wondering vaguely where the intervening days had gone that suddenly the big event was looming.

The 'limo' ordered for Meegan was calling for her first and would be here in half an hour. She longed for her mother, or a friend, to be with her. Someone to say, You look lovely, Sophie, in a way that would boost her flagging confidence.

The girl at the hairdresser's had been kind, assuring her that the slicked-back styling of her hair emphasised the good bones of her face and gave her a sculptured look.

I want to be pretty, not sculptured, she'd wanted to say, but couldn't reveal her insecurities to a stranger.

'This will emphasise your eyes,' another attendant had told her, brushing a mink-dark shadow across her eyelids. 'They are your best feature and you should make the most of them.'

Meegan had talked her into having her

make-up applied at the salon, mainly because she wanted hers done as well and needed Sophie's moral support. The pair of them had gazed at their transformations in silence, then Meegan had given her great peal of laughter.

'Don't look so amazed, Sophie,' she had said. 'We'll both be back to normal tomorrow!'

But would she ever be back to normal? she wondered as she walked carefully down the stairs to wait for the car in the quiet foyer of the flats.

'I was about to ring,' a deep voice told her, and she looked through the glass and saw Cal standing there, looking so very handsome in his dinner-suit that she wanted to cry.

'I—I thought the car was picking me up,' she stammered, not knowing how to behave in the new shell that surrounded her.

'I came with it in case the driver needed a hand with the wheelchairs,' he told her. 'Are you going to open the door and let me in, or will you eventually come out?'

She took the necessary step forward, and pulled open the door, then felt his hand reach out and touch her arm.

'You look so beautiful it takes my breath away,' he said very quietly.

'I—I thought the same about you,' she stammered, then blushed at her gaucherie.

'Shall we go to the ball, Cinderella?' he asked, bowing low in front of her.

'I suppose we should or Meegan will be getting anxious,' she replied, battling to settle her flighty nerves and leaping heart.

He took her arm, and the feel of his skin on hers fired her body and there were no words left that she could hide behind, no hope of any further pretence.

Helping her into the car, he maintained an impersonal touch, then slid in beside the driver and gave directions in a low-voiced murmur. Had he sensed her reaction to him and withdrawn as a result of it? Uncertainty provoked a misery that threatened to cloud the evening, and she felt a wave of exasperation at the uncontrolled mood swings she was experiencing.

Meegan's ethereal beauty, enhanced by the silver gown, was emphasised by her dark-suited escorts, waiting patiently, one each side of her, in the car park outside the motel.

Their excitement broke the tension in the

air, and the babble of conversation, the clutter of compliments, carried them to the big house at Seafish Cove, where lights and music spilled out to welcome them.

'You two will be the stars of the evening,' Mrs Williams announced as she came forward to greet them. 'I've dressed the women in this town for thirty years, but never have I had two that did more justice to my clothes!'

Linking one arm through Sophie's elbow, and taking Meegan by the hand, she led them into the house, whirling them around the guests in a flurry of introductions that Sophie had no hope of remembering.

Beautiful women, exquisitely clad, dotted the room, and the men in their dinner-suits added to the festive air. Sophie found a glass of champagne pressed into her hand, and smiled at a man who appeared by her side, opening up the conversation with a question about how long she had been in Westport. He reminded her of Dr Crane and she chatted easily, acknowledging the introductions as other people appeared to join them. She forced herself to look at the faces of each speaker, stopping her eyes from flickering around the room in a tell-tale search for the one person she wanted by her side. Swallowing some champagne for Dutch courage, she smiled and laughed and responded to the chatter so that it seemed as if only minutes had passed before they were being shuffled back into cars to go on to the ball.

Grant Stokes appeared and she greeted him with a warm, genuine smile, pleased to find one familiar face in the group.

'Do you want a lift?' he asked, and she shook her head, explaining about staying with Meegan in case she needed a hand. She looked around quite casually, wondering if Cal would come with their party again, but could not see his broad back or dark head in the shifting, shuffling crowd.

'Let's go!' Gerald said, taking her arm and leading her towards the door where Meegan and Mark waited for the car to pull forward. 'It's good fun so far, isn't it?' he asked with the simple sincerity that Sophie found so disarming.

'Great fun,' she agreed, surprising even herself when she realised she meant it. She would have a wonderful night, she decided, whatever happened. What had Mrs Williams said about letting the other

Sophies come out and enjoy themselves?

'Let's go,' she said to the driver. 'We've a ball waiting for us.'

'For someone who can't dance, you seem to have done remarkably well.'

Cal's voice slid into her ears as she dropped into a chair beside Meegan after a particularly energetic half-hour on the dance-floor with Gerald. He was sitting in the semicircle of chairs behind her, but she could feel his shoulder brush against her bare arm and almost taste him as she breathed in the unique aroma she associated with him.

'All you do is stand on the floor and wriggle to the music,' she told him loftily, with an unconcern she was far from feeling.

His mother had introduced one man after another, all eager, it seemed, to show her how to do the latest dances, and chuckle at her mistakes as she gyrated round the floor. It *had* been fun but only iron control had stopped her constantly seeking him out with her eyes, hurting herself with images of him in the arms of beautiful women.

'And you wriggle most attractively, I thought,' he continued in a mock-serious voice. 'Will you try it with me after this break?'

'I suppose I could,' she replied calmly, while her foolish heart jiggled about in her chest and her last remaining shred of self-protective instinct warned her that he was only being polite.

'I—I'm not up to this kind of dancing,' she stuttered, when he led her on to the dance-floor and pulled her into his arms. She shuddered at the contact and tried to twist away, but the arms that held her tightened, so that she felt the whole length of his body pressed against her.

'Humour me!' he whispered in her ear, guiding her effortlessly around the dance-floor, making her legs move in unison with his through the warm, insistent pressure of his thighs.

Time hung suspended like a bright golden balloon as they moved as one across the floor, music flooding her senses and love flooding her soul. Could one person feel so much emotion if the other did not reciprocate?

The question tumbled into her mind, then tumbled out again as Cal's head bent closer and his lips brushed against her neck, starting a fierce fire that raced through her blood, swelling her breasts with a strange heaviness and sending tingling waves of sweet desire shooting up her legs and into the core of her being.

'You've been the belle of the ball, you realise,' he said as the music stopped and she moved apart.

'Ornamental enough to hang on your sleeve?' she asked huskily, knowing she shouldn't, yet unable to stop herself.

'Ornamental enough for anyone's sleeve.'

Something in his voice made her look up into his face, and the seriousness of his expression frightened her.

'At least you've met most of the eligible men about town. I guess they'll all be beating a path to your door!'

'Oh, I'm sure they will,' she said lightly, shrugging to hide the spasm of pain stabbing through her with his words.

'That's good,' he said, his eyes as cool and clear as glass. 'You've a bit of lost time to make up in the games that men and women play.'

Is that all it is? A game? she wanted to cry, but tears would blotch her make-up and she was too old to cry anyway.

'I'll do my best,' she promised him, hoping her lips weren't trembling enough to give the lie to her calmness.

'Good,' he murmured, then leant forward and kissed her on the cheek. 'Good luck, Sophie!' he added softly, then he turned his back and walked away.

It had been goodbye! So why was she still trying to convince herself of that eight weeks later?

She threw herself into her work, trying to find the solace it had once offered. Mrs Carstairs' melanoma had been removed, but malignancy had been found in her lymph system and she was undergoing radiation therapy at the local hospital. Sophie watched her courage and determination, praying for a little of it to help her through this phase of her life.

'For it will pass!' she kept telling herself. 'You're a doctor, and you know people don't die of a broken heart!'

At first she refused invitations from men she had met at the ball, afraid that Cal might phone or call in. She drifted round to the motel, time and time again, telling herself it was useless but unable to control the urge that forced her to go, but now that work on the house had started Meegan, Mark and Gerald saw Cal most days at the estate, and after a while hearing his name on their lips hurt more than not hearing it.

'Have dinner with me tonight, before I go on duty?' Grant asked the question when he met her on the steps of the clinic as she started work one morning. 'Wind's from the west so there's no surf!'

'I'd like that,' she said quickly, before she had time to think of an excuse not to go. 'But surely you don't surf at night anyway?'

He smiled his clear, flashing smile. 'If I'm surfing all day, I sleep up until it's time to leave for work,' he explained. 'I'll call by your place at seven.'

It was easy, she decided later, this going out business—and enjoyable! If only because, for two and a half hours, she had no time at all to think about Cal Williams.

'Yes, I'd like that,' became her catchphrase as she accepted the invitations that came her way, slowly gaining confidence in her ability to chat politely over dinner, slowly accepting the attractive butterfly disguise that had emerged from the plump chrysalis she'd lived in for so long.

It was easy if she ignored the hollow feeling inside her, and the emptiness she felt when she returned, alone, to her flat after each night out. Even easier if she could slip away from an escort without a hot, wet kiss pressed on her lips, or an intrusive arm slipped around her shoulders, and soft endearments she didn't want to hear whispered in her ear.

'Enjoying Westport now?' Janet Williams asked her when they met at an art show one evening.

'Very much,' Sophie replied untruthfully, avoiding the grey eyes that were searching her face.

'Love's like measles!' the older woman said, shocking Sophie into looking at her, a puzzled question in her eyes.

'It's an old saying, or a quote or something,' she explained. 'Something about getting it worse if you're older. You're a doctor; you'd know about that.'

'Doctors don't cover love in their course!' Sophie told her, angry with the woman for pressing on the bruise that was her heart.

'I meant measles!' Janet said, patting her on the arm. 'You'd know if you get them worse when you're older. I think he meant well,' she added obscurely, then walked away, leaving Sophie gazing after her, a frown flickering between her eyes as she tried to make sense of the conversation.

'I'm going out with the truck,' Gerald announced, sidling up to take Janet's place by her side.

Maybe it's me! Sophie thought, looking at the glass of mineral water in her hand and wondering if it was spiked. I can't seem to follow conversations any more.

'On Sunday,' Gerald continued. 'And Tim says there'd be room for someone else. Would you like to come?'

'I'm sorry, Gerald,' she began, and saw the disappointment cloud his face. 'Not sorry I can't go,' she assured him. 'I'm not working so whatever it is I'm sure I'd love to go, but I don't remember about the truck.'

'The pigeon truck, Sophie,' he explained. 'The truck that lets the pigeons go so they can race home. All the owners put their pigeons in baskets on the truck, and a man drives them out into the bush and lets them all go. They fly home and their owners have whistles to call them back down into their yards.'

If tenacity and single-mindedness made a good pigeon breeder, then Gerald would succeed, Sophie decided, smiling ruefully at the thought of Sunday's outing. Maybe Cal Williams had been right to encourage Gerald to reach beyond the limits she would have set for him.

'We have to leave early, five o'clock!' he told her. 'The driver is picking me up and then I'll tell him your address. The pigeons don't like to fly when it's too hot.'

'You learning about pigeons too?' Mark joined them and Sophie nodded.

'And think how much more I'll know after however many hours it will be in the truck with *two* pigeon-fanciers!'

Five o'clock Sunday was cold and blustery, although the rain that was threatening still hung in the low clouds. Sophie pulled her warm jacket closer round her shoulders and shivered. She was debating whether to walk back inside the foyer and wait, when a decrepit old truck wheezed and coughed its way around the corner and pulled up at the kerb.

'You sit in the middle, Sophie!' Gerald told her, hopping down from his seat and holding the door. Noises from under the tar-paulin at the back told her that the pigeons were already loaded, so she smiled at Gerald's excitement and clambered up into the dingy cabin.

'Good morning, Sophie!'

His voice was hoarse, as if he had a cold, and his grey eyes were swiftly hooded when she searched his face, feasting on the familiar features like a starving man on food.

'You drive the pigeon truck?' she croaked, still half way into her seat.

'Only today,' he told her, with a silly little smile twisting his lips. 'The driver was sick and Gerald had set his heart on going, so I offered.'

'Hurry up, Sophie!' Gerald called, but she was unable to move, unwilling to slide across the seat and bring her body into con-tact with his.

'I didn't know he'd asked you until I picked him up at the motel,' Cal explained, and Sophie felt the pain twist in her heart.

You wouldn't have come if you had, she thought, and tried to back out past Gerald's leg and hip, now pushing her across the seat towards Cal.

'Don't disappoint him,' he murmured, and she stopped resisting, so her body slid across the seat, coming to rest against the warmth of his, feeling his leg and hip through the fine wool of her trousers, hard and hot against her chilled skin.

'This is a short flight,' Gerald explained, and she forced herself to respond normally. 'How have you learnt so much so quickly?'

'I wanted to know about it so I can keep pigeons, and people like Mr Phillips and Cal are helping me, so I have to try to learn it quickly so I don't take up too much of their time and become a nuisance.'

'You could never be a nuisance, Gerald,' Cal said quickly, but Sophie was struck by something special in his words, an element of philosophy that she couldn't quite grasp, but that she was certain applied equally to non-disabled people.

'People are a nuisance if they don't try to do things for themselves!' Gerald stated definitely, and Sophie repeated the word 'nuisance' in her head, and knew it was correct. Not cowardly, just a nuisance! Was this the philosophy that had shaped Mark's repatriation? Had she been a nuisance to her family over the years, not trying to control her eating, not making any effort to go out with the young men they paraded in front of her?

She had met Cal Williams' attempts to be friendly with open suspicion. Had he drifted away because she was a nuisance?

She shifted uncomfortably. Gerald had stopped talking and drifted off to sleep, and her thoughts, and the silence, were becoming unendurable.

'Enjoying Westport, are you?' Cal asked quietly.

'Your mother asked me that the other day,' she said, not knowing what else to say.

'And did you answer her?' he asked, with the gentle, teasing mockery that was part of what she loved in him.

'Not truthfully,' she told him, shifting uncomfortably in her cramped space.

'But you've met plenty of people, been getting about, going out with——'

The question was cut off abruptly, and he concentrated on the rough road that led up through the scrub behind the town.

The silence descended again, but Sophie did not mind as a feeling of contentment stole through her. There was something so right about sitting here, squeezed up against his warm, bulky body like this. Was there any harm in just enjoying it for the day?

She slid easily into a peaceful daydream, snuggling her head on to his shoulder as sleep set her dreams free.

'Fine company on a trip you two are!' Cal was saying gruffly, when the cessation of the rumbling movement woke her.

'Are we there already?' she asked, opening her eyes to find him looking down at her with a strange expression on his face.

'Already?' he teased, with the funny little quirky smile she loved so much. 'You've been asleep for three hours, and Gerald's still asleep.'

'We're there? At the place where we let the pigeons go?'

He nodded, still smiling, as if he found her confusion amusing.

'We'll have to wake Gerald. Do you know what to do?'

Now she was panicking, not because of the pigeons, although that would do for a cover, but because his presence here beside her was sending riotous messages through her body—vestiges of the dream, she kept telling herself, sternly resisting the urge to lean forward just a little, to reach up, just a fraction, and let her lips. . .

'Wake up properly, Sophie!' he snapped, and his voice wasn't gently teasing any more!

Then the door opened, cold air flooded into the space where he had been and she shook herself out of the dangerous lethargy. Gerald was now awake, hurrying out to help Cal with the release mechanisms that would free the birds.

'What's the time?' Cal demanded as she dropped down to the ground and looked around.

'Nine-fifteen.'

I can still respond to orders, she thought hazily, breathing in the eucalypt-laden air and jumping up and down to warm her feet.

'We have to make a note of the time we let them go,' Gerald explained kindly.

The two men disappeared around the back of the truck, pulling at the tarpaulin cover, then fiddling with metal bars.

'Time now, Sophie?'

'Nine-twenty!' she told him, and watched in awe as the birds rose into the air, circled lazily, then headed off, unerringly seeking out their homes hundreds of miles away.

'Isn't it great?' Gerald asked, his face alight with joy and wonder.

'Great!' Sophie agreed, smiling warmly at him then tilting back her head to watch the birds diminish into distant specks in the blue sky.

'Great!' a deep voice said close by her side, his eyes not on the birds but on her upturned face. She felt a flush of heat rise to flood her cheeks when she saw the admiration—and something else, quickly hidden?—in his expression.

'Let's go!'

He turned away, breaking the spell that had bound them for an instant, and Sophie knew it was no good. Whatever he felt for her, it wasn't love. Love couldn't be so cold, so cruel, so uncaring!

They squashed back into the truck, and set off for home in silence, Gerald too entranced by what he'd seen to want to speak, and Sophie too depressed by the sudden revelation she'd experienced.

The old truck, lightened of its load, rattled over the dusty roads at a good pace, jostling their bodies together in a feigned intimacy that made her grit her teeth with the effort to remain rigidly apart.

Twisting among trees, it crept up a low hill, then picked up speed on the downward slope, so they had little chance of stopping when the big red steer burst out of a lane and on to the road in front of them. Cal spun the wheel, steering the truck into the bank at the side of the road in an effort to avoid the inevitable collision, but the wheels skidded on the gravel and the cabin tipped eerily, then spun around in a whirling confusion of red hide, dust, trees and tumbling bodies.

'Sophie, are you all right? Sophie, answer me, darling; look at me, tell me you're OK.'

The voice was urgent, beseeching, desperate!

She opened her eyes and saw Cal's face, bent close to hers, white and anxious.

'I love you,' she said, and smiled, then closed her eyes again.

'You're concussed,' he told her angrily, shaking her awake again. But it was gentle anger! 'I want to get you out of here. I'm worried about fire. Do you hurt anywhere? Can I move you? You're a doctor, Sophie! I need your help.'

'I can get out,' she told him, and tried to

move, gasping aloud as she felt pain shoot up her leg. 'I'm all right,' she assured him, seeing his face whiten even more, and the grim set of his lips. 'My ankle is hurt, but I wouldn't be able to feel it if I had spinal injuries. How's Gerald?'

She eased herself up a little, and felt his warm, strong arms reach out to enfold her.

'I've got Gerald out,' he told her. 'Now, is your ankle stuck? I don't want to make it worse by trying to get you out if it's wedged in there.'

He's being so calm and sensible that I should help him, Sophie thought, wanting only to relax back into those comforting arms and go to sleep.

'Sophie? Don't faint on me again. Not yet!' he ordered in a strained voice.

'I'm fine!' she told him, although the pain in her ankle when she moved her leg was like a red-hot poker being thrust through her skin. 'And I'm not stuck.'

He lifted her out, carrying her as gently as he could across to the shade of a tree, where Gerald lay, pale and still.

The sight of him restored more brain cells to working order.

'Is he bleeding anywhere?' she asked urgently, but she couldn't remember why it was important.

'No, but he's unconscious. He has a bump on his head where he probably came forward and hit the windscreen.'

'We must get help for him, Cal. Now!' she urged, although she still didn't know what was worrying her so much.

'I can't leave you here,' he said in an anguished voice. 'Someone will come before long; they can go for help.'

'You've got to go,' she insisted. 'You've got to go now. Look!' She pointed over to the fence where cattle had gathered to peer enquiringly at them. 'There's a horse over there; you're a cowboy. You can ride for help.'

She started to giggle weakly, then tried to stop when she saw the frown darkening Cal's face, but somehow she couldn't stop and the laughter turned to tears.

'You've got to go,' she sobbed, while he squatted on the ground beside her, drawing her into his arms and stroking her hair while he murmured silly things about love and never leaving her again and not caring if it was unfair because she was so inexperienced—he'd had enough of doing the right thing.

'You've got to go; it's help for Gerald and I know it's important,' she told him again, when the tears had stopped for long enough for her to speak. 'Please go, Cal, please go!' she begged, and recognised the dreadful pain that tore at him before he drew his arms away from her and set off at a jog down the road they had been following.

For what seemed like hours she watched Gerald's white face while an unrecognisable dread grew within her. Then a car pulled up and Cal was back by her side, talking about ambulances and love and wasted time, while she slid out of consciousness again.

'It's Noonan Syndrome,' she told the startled ambulance attendant, trying to sit up on the stretcher as they wound their way through traffic on the freeway. Gerald lay beside her, as white and still as she had last seen him, although now an oxygen mask covered half his face.

'Gerald has NS and there's a common blood deficiency in factors eight, nine and twelve.'

The man looked at her blankly. Did her know nothing?

'Where's Cal?' she demanded. 'I must speak to Cal.'

'You'll be right. You can talk to him when we get to the hospital,' the attendant soothed.

'But I might faint again,' she cried, twisting against the straps that held her prisoner. 'I must tell him.'

'I'll tell him,' the man assured her.

'Tell him factors eight, nine and twelve and maybe others,' she fretted, feeling her brain scrambling again as she tried to make the words sound more sensible. 'And maybe others but definitely abnormal factors.'

'I'll tell him! I'll tell him!'

The words echoed in her mind as she was wheeled through the emergency entrance at the large hospital where she had trained.

'Tell who what?' a smiling head enquired, blocking out the bright light as it hovered above her.

'Tell Cal about Gerald,' she said crossly, then recognised the face as that of a registrar she had known for years.

'Peter?'

'Spot-on! You can't be as concussed as you sound. You're on your way to X-Ray but I'd say you've a broken ankle. Your little mate's being watched because he's still unconscious.'

'And Cal?'

'Only two of you came in, Sophie,' Peter told her, and she felt the tears slide down her cheeks as frustration and loneliness clashed together in her tortured mind.

'There, there,' he said, awkwardly patting her shoulder, but she shrugged against the comfort as she battled to recall what was so important—or even why it was important.

'Can I see Gerald?' she cried, and, as if anxious to appease her, Peter nodded, and told the orderly to wheel her into the side-room where he lay.

It was the ashen colour that reminded her, and all the cogs in her mind clicked into place.

'He's probably a bleeder,' she said urgently. 'Internal haemorrhage! It's part of Noonan Syndrome, easy bruising and abnormal clotting factors in the blood.'

'Eight, nine and twelve,' Peter said, grabbing a blood-pressure cuff and winding it round Gerald's arm as he spoke. 'The ambulance attendant said you insisted on telling someone those numbers—he'd forgotten the factor part of it, if you told him!'

He pushed her wheeled bed aside to get to the door.

'Anti-shock trousers, in here now!' he called down the hall then returned to Gerald's side to draw up blood. 'And a runner to take this to Pathology for typing,' he said to the nurse who appeared with the shock garment. 'And some warmed plasma to start fluid resuscitation, and some AHF.'

'Prothrombinex has factor nine,' Sophie told him, pleased that her brain seemed to be working again.

'You leave him to me,' Peter told her. 'You've done your bit!'

The nurse returned and he asked her to find an orderly to take Sophie to X-Ray.

'And tell everyone she's a VIP and to be treated accordingly. Phone through to Dr Craig and let him know it's Dr Delano, and he'll come down and set her ankle personally, I suspect.'

He blew Sophie a kiss and turned back to his patient, his mind already on the measures he must take to save Gerald's life.

Sophie smiled as she was wheeled away, and, certain that her friend was in good hands, she let the pain she'd held at bay wash over her as lights and voices receded into blankness.

'Cal?'

'Hello, Sophie!'

The words were deep and tender, but a hint of roughness made her frown, searching his almost stern face as she struggled back to reality.

'Is Gerald all right?' she demanded, thinking the worst.

'Not yet, but they think he'll pull through, thanks to your insistence on repeating numbers at everyone who looked at you.'

He smiled at her, the skin at the corner of his mouth tugging upwards—a little reluctantly, she thought.

'If Gerald's OK, why do you look so miserable?' she begged as something inside her began to shake. 'Or are you here to say goodbye again and walk away from me?' she cried, wanting so much to touch him, to feel his skin, and bones and muscle, and have him hold her close, and whisper 'Sophie' as he had in a dream she vaguely remembered.

'I won't walk away again,' he said, his

velvety voice stroking soothingly across her skin. 'Won't walk away because I can't.'

He spread his hands and shrugged his shoulders, but still he didn't touch her, and still she trembled with a fearful dread.

'Won't walk away because I can't, Doctor, darling,' he repeated, the funny little smile she loved so much twisting his lips. 'If you want me to go, you'll have to send me,' he finished, and looked down at her with eyes so full of what looked like love, she felt stupid hot tears prickle behind her eyelids.

'Wh-why would I want to send you away?' she stammered. 'Why would I ever want to do that?'

'So you can meet other men, learn a little more about life and love and men and women. Your inexperience shattered me, Sophie. Knowing no one before me, how could you judge your feelings? How could you find out if what you feel for me is really love or just a first mad, wild infatuation?'

'Then you know how I feel?' she demanded, angry that he was torturing them both like this.

'I kind of guessed there might be some attraction when I first kissed you, Sophie. People don't usually meet and kiss like that unless there's something pretty strong at work between them. It hit me just as hard, you know,' he told her wryly, 'and shook me pretty badly.'

He turned away, and she saw again the clean-cut profile and angled jaw that had haunted her dreams.

'I rather fancied myself as a man of the world, beyond all that romantic love nonsense,' he continued, turning back to face her with a serious expression on his face. 'For years I'd taken out different women, enjoying their company but not finding that elusive magic other people called love, until, at last, I had begun to think it was all a fantasy. Then you erupted on to that hillside and I picked you up and felt a crazy, mad, incredible reaction that I tried to pretend was fear for your safety. I wanted to kiss you right there and then,' he admitted, smiling widely now, as if inviting her to share the silly joke.

'I thought you didn't like me and kept kissing me because you thought I might be chasing you,' Sophie mumbled, wondering if maybe she was still a little concussed, because now what she had thought didn't seem to make sense.

'Oh, Doctor, darling,' he whispered, his hand moving to touch her arm, and lighting the fires that she'd thought had died forever into flames beneath her skin. 'I kissed you because I couldn't stop myself,' he said. 'There you were, arms outflung on my own special bit of hillside, looking like a dark spirit come down to earth to taunt me with that still, mysterious beauty I'd only glimpsed earlier.'

She reached across and covered his hand with her own, not daring to move closer or feel more of him in case all the torrents of fire that burnt within her were suddenly unleashed in an uncontrollable conflagration.

'Can't stop myself now, either,' he said at last, and she felt his hand move on her skin and then his arm was sliding round her, drawing her close as he half sat on the bed, and he bent his head to touch her lips.

'Oh, Cal!' she breathed against his mouth, and tried to snuggle closer, to feel more and more of him. 'Aaggh!' she cried as pain jerked her mind away from passion and she looked, for the first time, to the end of the bed, where her ankle, heavily plastered, and strung above the bed in traction, was throbbing with an unrelenting agony.

'Oh, Sophie! Now I've hurt you!'

The words were muffled as his dark head bent into the side of the bed and his hands clenched tightly in his hair.

'I hurt myself trying to move,' she told him as the pain eased and she settled herself back down against the pillows.

The moment was lost, but she sensed it was her turn. Carefully, she reached out and threaded her fingers through his hair, touching the warmth of his hands as they slowly relaxed.

'After the accident, did you ride off on that horse to get help?' she asked, and was rewarded by his head lifting and a shamefaced grin.

'The Cowboy is a nickname the kids at school gave me,' he admitted. 'Comes from having a mother stupidly romantic enough to name me after the town where I was conceived!'

He was blushing, she decided, this Don Juan, this Casanova! Actually blushing!

'Not from riding roughshod over people's dreams?' she teased, and he shook his head, his grey eyes glistening and his lips almost twitching into a smile.

'Or from any skill with horses,' he admitted, finally letting the smile break across his face. 'I haven't ridden a horse since my merry-go-round days!'

'Oh, Cal!' she murmured, and somehow she knew it was all going to be all right, because he was touching her again, patting her arm, and pressing his fingers deep into her flesh, with a hunger as real as that which she saw in his face and felt burning through her own body.